© Ian Drawie 2020.

To Bomber and the rest of my mates in F-Troop with amusement.

EARLY DAYS

"Awoooooooo," I cried, as I began working on this book. Not because I am 'bark raving mad', though there are many people who think I am, but because working on this autobiography brought back many memories of the days when I was leader of Millwall's notorious F-Troop – the hardest football hooligan firm in the 1970s. It was such a far cry from my early days.

I was born at home, number 12 Delmark Street, in Millwall on the isle of Dogs, on the 4th January 1959. My father, Albert Dog was a plumber who had fought with the Desert Rats at El Alamein, and my mother Annie Dog, was a cleaning lady who worked in an office down the road.

Like most children in my street, I was not an only child. My brother, Charlie, was two years older than I was, and my sister, Lucy, a good five years older.

I can't say I have many memories of the first five years in this world, what kid does, but I can remember being taken to the local park in the pram and visiting my grandparents, Elsa and Tommy Dog, who lived across the road from us, at number 21 Delmark Street. But that's just about it.

Still, all that changed when I started at Wilboro Infants School and found myself in the assembly hall listening to the headmaster, a weedy looking man called Hatcher. He welcomed us to the school and told us what we could expect to learn at the school in the years ahead. Then, when he had finished rabbiting on, we had to listen as one teacher after another stepped forward and began reading out a list of names. When your name was called you had to get up and stand behind the teacher along with all the other kids whose names were called, and that was how you found out what class you were in and who your classmates were.

So there I was, listening as a stern looking lady with glasses began reading out a list of names: Roy Thompson, Peter Fairbanks, David Crossland, Graham Turner, and as she did all the kids got up and stood behind her and nobody made any comment. Then she yelled Harry Dog and before I had even risen to my feet, some overweight blob with greasy hair yelled, "Harry Dog, ha ha ha, look everybody we have a dog in our school."

Well there was laughter all round and I was so angry I ran over and kicked the fat blob so hard in his face, his eyes nearly popped out of his head and I wasn't finished yet. I kicked him in the balls and then began jumping up and down on his head. I would have continued but before I could do so, the teachers had pulled me off him and I was taken kicking and screaming to Mr Hatcher's office.

Once there, I was expecting to have my backside slapped, as my brother Charlie had told me that's what happened to kids who stepped out of line and were taken to the headmaster's office, but I wasn't. I was simply given a firm telling off and allowed to join my class.

I think the headmaster thought it was all over and in fact I'm sure he did, but it wasn't. That fat kid had tried to humiliate me and there was no way I was going to let him get away with it even though I had already given him a good kicking. So, I watched him go into the boys' toilets before following him in and punching him so hard in the face he now had a second black eye to match the one he already had. Then I grabbed him by the throat and told him if he ever made fun of me again, or my name, I would see he regretted it.

"Got it?" I said clenching my fists.

"Yeah," he cried sobbing his eyes out. "I've got it."

I never had any problems from that little weasel again and indeed it wasn't long before word got round that I wasn't a kid you messed about with and not just at school either. My best mates at school were Tommy Sims, Gary Roberts, and Peter Winterbourne and we called ourselves Harry's Gang because I was their leader. What's more we were a very multicultural gang, because Gary Roberts, or Robo as I called him, was as black as the ace of spades, which often led to some other kids digging us out and wanting to know why we were mixing with a nigger.

Now this was not a problem at infant school because most of the kids were black or of Asian heritage, but when I moved to St David's Junior school all that changed.

The school was right next to the Levin Estate and that was riddled with poor white working-class families with links to the National Front (NF) British Movement, and other such racist scum. Indeed the local NF organiser Tommy Richardson lived there and one day we were walking down Wickmore Street when he pulled up in his car and beckoned me over.

"Hey kid. Come here I want a word with you."

I went over and he leaned forward and grabbed me by the throat.

"Why are you mixing with that nigger?" he said, glancing coldly at Robo. "We don't tolerate race mixers round here."

"No," I said, coldly. "Well I don't give a fuck. I'll mix with who I like, got it."

Well Richardson's eyes nearly popped out of his head and the three skinheads behind him burst out laughing in disbelief. Before I knew, it he had slapped me across the face sending me tumbling over some bins and leaving me somewhat bog eyed on the floor.

"Learn some manners kid," he yelled, before driving away, "or next time it will be curtains for you."

The next day Richardson was in his local boozer laughing and chatting away when I walked in and casually strolled over to him. I was carrying a baseball bat and when he turned round I smashed it into his face leaving him lying on the floor with blood pouring down his face.

"Touch me again, you bastard, and I'll be back with my grandfather's shotgun and I will blow your fucking head off, got it?" With that I walked away leaving him flat out on the floor and everybody looking at me in astonishment.

Well that wasn't the end of it, as I knew it wouldn't be. A week later I saw him following me, so I walked down to the docks and then continued until I came to some derelict buildings. Once upon a time over a thousand men and women had worked here helping load goods on and off the ships, but those days had long gone and the buildings had gone to ruin. Still I wasn't here to dwell on the past but to deal with an annoying little weasel, so I went inside the building and took my grandfather's shotgun, which I had been carrying around with me in the expectation Richardson would come after me, out of my school bag.

As soon as he entered, I fired the gun above his head sending him scurrying to the floor in blind panic. I wasn't finished yet. I quickly reloaded and put the shotgun to his head.

"No don't shoot, Harry," he yelled begging for his life. "I'm sorry for hitting you, I really am."

"That's as may be," I said, calmly. "But you were warned if you touched me again I would blast you with my shotgun and now you have followed me here, so what am I to do?"

"Oh but I wasn't going to lay a finger on you Harry," he pleaded. "I just wanted to tell you that I bore you no hard feelings, and that as far as I'm concerned I will not bother you again."

"Bollocks," I replied. "You could have told me that when you first saw me. You wouldn't have followed me down here to tell me that. You only did that because you intended to hurt me in some way."

I cocked my weapon and he screamed and again started begging for mercy and what a pathetic sight he was. I mean here was a member of the so-called master race, as he and his NF mates would have you believe, and here he was whimpering like a little baby. Still, luckily for him I had no intention of killing him. I mean what would have been the point. It would only be a matter of time before somebody would tell the police about the incident in the pub and that would be it. They would be round to my house quicker than you could say hey presto and I would have been arrested on the spot. So, I told him that this was his final warning and if he ever harassed me again, I would kill him.

Well he assured me he wouldn't, but to be honest I had my doubts. After all the man was a thug and thugs never like being made to look small, particularly by an

11-year-old kid like me. I needn't have worried about repercussions, however, because unbeknown to me the man had attacked a black youth by the name of Delroy Howard the day before, putting him in hospital, and Delroy's dad wanted revenge.

So, after I told him to piss off and he had fled back home, the dad was waiting for him and stabbed him repeatedly in the abdomen killing him instantly.

So as I said, I needn't have worried about any repercussions because now the bastard was dead there wouldn't be any would there, well not against me anyway. His NF mates might want revenge against the man who killed him, but that was his problem, not mine. If however, they chose to make it mine that would be another matter, and one which would probably end up with me getting my grandfather's shotgun out and blasting away at them too.

MUSKWELL HIGH

One of the best things about my schooldays was that every summer we would go to Butlin's, and the summer of 1970 was no different. What was different though, was that this year we went to Bognor Regis on the south coast and not Pwllheli or one of the other Butlin's camps we had been to before, not that I was complaining.

The place, like every other Butlin's camp, had so many things to do I hardly knew where to begin. The only problem was I had nobody to do things with…

I mean I don't want to sound cruel, but both my brother and sister were major league bores. They liked nothing more than sitting next to my mum and dad at a table by the pool, with their heads in their books, instead of splashing about in the water or dancing away in the kid's disco that Butlin's put on every evening.

It was annoying at the best of times, but what was even more annoying was that my brother Charlie had a really irritating way of behaving and acting as though everybody should fall into line with his wishes. When he didn't get his way, or rather when I didn't give it to him, because everybody else in the family seemed to bow down to his every wish, he would sit there with his head down knowing my sister would come to his rescue.

She always did and about a week into the holiday I had had enough. The next time he sat there with his head bowed letting my sister do his bidding, I punched him hard in the face, and he fell back off the chair and was out for the count. Of course my sister kicked up a fuss but that wasn't a problem. I just punched her in the face too and that was it, she was out as well.

That September, I started at Muskwell High, and it wasn't long before I got into a fight. In fact, I got into a fight before I even got there because to get to the school, you had to walk under a subway tunnel, or at least you did if you were walking there from my house, and as I walked down into it I noticed a group of kids wearing the same uniform as me, smoking and talking amongst themselves. I didn't think anything of it until I walked past and one of them decided to flick his cigarette end at me. So, without warning I turned round and punched him so hard in the face, he hit the deck and was unconscious.

That was at 8.45 a.m. By 3.50 p.m., I was on my way home and had to pass under the same tunnel. As I went down I noticed the same lads I spotted this morning were there, only this time they weren't so much lounging about but waiting for me. I wasn't surprised. I had knocked one of them out and it was clear they would want revenge.

I had discovered that these kids were in the same year as me, and were the same age as me, because I had seen them in the assembly hall where all the new kids were gathering when I walked in. If they wanted a fight they were going to get one especially as I wasn't alone. Simsey, Robo, and Winto were with me.

So, without and warning I yelled, "Awoooooooo," before dashing forward and laying into them.

The lot of them looked surprised and began fighting back, but with me lashing out with my fists and boots, and Robo and the rest doing likewise it wasn't long before we had them on the run and they began to leg it as fast as their legs would take them. We gave chase but they got away, which wasn't a problem because the next day when they were walking to school we were waiting for them. This time they all wound up bog eyed on the floor, even though there were four of us, and six of them.

As so often happens in the first few weeks at a new school all the local hard cases wanted to show that they were cock of the year, so I spent the first two weeks, kicking, punching, and knocking out all potential rivals to the title. That wasn't hard because by now, I realised I had a punch that rivalled Mike Tyson's and often that was all it took to knock somebody out. Even if it wasn't, I would lay into them with such ferocity that they wished I had. In fact I was such a ferocious kid that I would lay into groups of people and not just one person on their own.

I can remember on one occasion when I was walking across the school field and a couple of older kids decided to dig me out.

"Hey Mugsy," one cried. "Do you see that kid there with the brown curly hair? That's the one that's always fighting, and he's the cock of the first year."

"Looks like a wimp to me," cried Mugsy giving me a cold stare.

"And you look like a fucking faggot to me," I cried, "you and your girlfriends here."

I was referring to the six lads with him who were staring at me with sneers on their faces and the moment I said it, those sneers vanished and all of them stepped towards me with clenched fists.

"Oh aye," I cried. "Fancy your chances do you? Well let's get to it." I threw my head back, and yelled, "Awoooooooo," before lunging into them one after another.

Well of course they were taken aback and being a lot bigger and older than I was, they fought back, but I wasn't deterred. No matter how many times they hit me or put me on the deck, I would get up and fight back, and when I did I was like a little Rottweiler tearing into them with every ounce of my strength. God knows how long it lasted, but it ended with them backing off and saying, "Enough kid enough. We're sorry we dug you out."

I had to smile at that because that was another way of saying I had won and they would never dig me out again, but even better one of them said, "Your name's Harry Dog isn't it?"

"Yeah,"

"Well it should be Harry the Dog because when you fight you fight like one hell of a wild dog and I mean one hell of a wild dog."

So that was how I came to be known as Harry the Dog, and if you're wondering why I had the rather odd habit of yelling, *Awoooooooo* before I hurled forward to attack opponents or whenever I got excited, then for that you have to thank Lon Chaney Jr.

You see my mother was a great fan of the man and liked nothing more than to watch his films every time they were on television or being shown down at the local pictures, and one day when I was five years old I was watching the Wolf Man when he suddenly let out a huge, "Awoooooooo," before transforming into a werewolf. And that was it, whenever I got excited or was about to lunge at someone, I too would throw my head back and yell, "Awoooooooo."

Sounds crazy I know but we all have our little idiosyncrasies do we not.

It wasn't just kids at my school who incurred my wrath when they stepped out of line though; kids from other schools did too, as one kid from Popular High found to his cost when we played them at football one cold Saturday in January 1972.

I was in the second year by then and getting bigger and stronger by the day. In fact I was five foot eight which was above average for somebody my age. What's more, I was a hell of a footballer. In fact I was so good that my PE teacher, Mr Thompson, would later write in my end of year report that I was the kid most likely to make it as a football player.

However, good or not, I was a fighter at heart as some blond-haired kid found to his cost on that cold winter's day.

It began when I took the ball from him fair and square. He tried to dribble it past me, but I stopped him and then passed it over to Winto on the right wing. I didn't think anything more about it, but then the blond-haired kid ran past me and spat in my face.

"What the fuck," I cried.

I watched him running down the field, with his head turned and he was looking at me with a sneer on his face. He wasn't sneering for long though. A couple of minutes later he was waiting for one of his mates to take a corner kick when he heard a loud, "Awoooooooo," and when he spun round in astonishment, he saw me glaring at him with my eyes narrowed and lips curled up in a grin. Then I lunged forward and headbutted him, and he wound up flat out on the ground and comatose.

I had another violent encounter on the pitch when I was in my third year, only this time it wasn't with somebody on the pitch, but somebody off it.

We were playing at home one Saturday and it was quite an intense game with neither side getting the better of the other, when this prat turned up and began making a nuisance of himself. When I say making a nuisance, what I meant was he didn't just start yelling words of encouragement to one side or another, as others watching the game from the touchline were doing. He began yelling abuse when somebody miskicked the ball, didn't shoot at the goal when he thought they should have, or failed to stop somebody when they dribbled past them and continued on forward.

In fact he was yelling so much abuse that everybody was getting fed up with him, including the referee, the opposition, and everybody else standing on the touchline. However, no matter how many times they told him to calm down and enjoy the game, he would either just ignore them or glare at them angrily until they backed off. In the end I felt compelled to say something so I went over and yelled, "Hey dickhead shut it. We're here to play football not listen to you rant and rave."

Well he didn't like that and went to take a swing at me, but I ducked and landed a punch on his gob, which send him reeling backwards and landing on the ground. He wasn't knocked out, which was unusual for somebody who had been punched by me, but neither did he want a fight, because he got up and ran off, leaving me and everybody else, including the referee laughing at him and thinking what a prat he was.

Still, we weren't laughing for long. About ten minutes later I was just about to take a corner kick, when Robo shouted, "For fuck sake Harry, look, that gobby git's back."

I wheeled round and couldn't believe my eyes. Not only was he back, he was carrying a sword. A large black samurai sword and I wondered where the hell he had got it from... But, if he thought it would scare me he was in for a surprise, because quick as a flash I pulled the corner post out of the ground and charged towards him. When I say charged towards him it was only after I had thrown my head in the air and yelled, "Awoooooooo," much to the surprise of both the spectators and the opposing team who had never heard anything like it before. I wasn't fazed by that, in fact I was like a medieval knight in a jousting competition rushing towards my opponent with a weapon in my hand. The only problem was he was no longer rushing at me with a weapon in his, but fleeing in the direction he had come.

I couldn't believe it when he suddenly turned and fled on his heels. This time though, I did not just stand there and laugh at him, but instead went chasing after him but it was to no avail. The man got away, and even though the police were called in by the school he was never traced. So who he was, what he was doing in Millwall that day, and where he fled to is anybody's guess. The only thing the police did establish is that this fool had nicked the sword from the shed of an elderly resident on a nearby estate, who for some reason kept it in there, before coming back to the school and rushing across the grass towards me with it clutched in his hand.

Whoever that idiot was, one thing was clear, he was a very lucky man that day. If I had caught up with him, I would have chopped off his head with the sword, shoved it on the end of the flagpole I was carrying, and hung it on the goal post, as a reminder to others not to piss me off and come charging at me with a sword, because if they did they were very likely to get beheaded. And ... this is precisely what Hatchet Harry of the Derby Lunatic Fringe did to two members of West Ham's Intercity Firm a couple of years later.

By the time I was in my fourth year, I was as strong as an ox, six foot one, and proving a hit with the girls in more ways than one. In fact I had always proved a hit with the girls in one form or another, but if truth be told I was a bit shy around them so nothing had really come of it. Can you believe that? The hardest kid around and shy of girls?

Still, that all changed when I got to my fourth year and I don't know whether that was because of adolescence, or because I was now tall and getting more confident by the day, or both. But, whatever the reason I was proving a hit with them as events at the local youth club showed.

In those days, unlike today, there was no Internet or many of the other things kids spend their time on, so instead they used to hang out at the local youth club, which the local council ran to keep the kids off the street and out of mischief. It was a great idea because there was so much to do that me and the rest of the crew were down there most nights, either playing snooker, table tennis, or indulging in one of the other pastimes kids liked to spend their time doing.

What made our youth club particularly enticing however; was that every Tuesday night they used to hold a kid's disco, which attracted kids from all over Millwall and some very strange kids at that.

The 1970s has often been described as quite tame compared to the Swinging Sixties but trust me the decade was not. In fact if anything it was more vibrant in terms of sex, violence, and, certainly, dress sense. I used to turn up wearing jeans, a white shirt, a coat, and trainers, you know casual stuff, but some of the kids would turn up dressed as mods, punks, and even goths, with black on their eyelids and lips and looking like they were something out of a freak show. But my all time favourite was this girl called Wendy, who liked to dress up as a witch as did several of her mates. They turned up at the disco wearing black dresses and cloaks, with long pointed hats and even holding wands.

The first time I saw her I said to her, "What the fuck are you doing with that? Are you fucking mad or what?"

She laughed, and said, "No, but if you don't buy me a drink Harry, I will cast a spell over you and turn you into a frog."

Well now it was my turn to laugh and I said to her, "How the fuck do you know my name?"

She just giggled and said, "You're Harry the Dog, and everybody knows who you are."

Well that was true, so I bought her a drink, or rather a glass of orange juice. As we were kids the bar would not serve us alcohol, because of the licensing laws and the fact that the council was running the club. Still that wasn't a problem because as I said I bought her a glass of orange, which turned out to be her favourite drink and after I put on the charm, we started dating. So, Wendy Harris, to give you her full name, became my first ever girlfriend and what a time we had.

We used to go to the pictures on a Saturday and snog on the back row as couples do, or go for walks in the park holding hands as we went. It was lovely and I was perhaps happier then than I was at any time during my life, but then fate intervened. Her father got a job in Scotland and within a month she had up sticked, and moved. I was devastated of course and we did write, but that fizzled out and that was it she was gone from my life and things were never quite the same.

Before she had left, however, we had made love in a barn and I had taken her virginity as she had taken mine. The result was I quickly discovered I liked sex just as much as I liked violence and I spent the rest of my fourth year shagging any bird I fancied.

Then I began my fifth year at school and it wasn't long before I found myself in a fight again. I was cock of the school and everybody knew it but then this new lad called Graham Tompkinson started and all that changed. He was from Liverpool and had been cock of his school in Kirby and it wasn't long before our paths crossed.

It began when Robo accidently bumped into him in the corridor. Robo apologised but instead of letting it go, Tompkinson tore into him with his boots and fists and put him on the floor eventually fracturing one of his ribs. I was off school with a heavy cold when I heard, but nonetheless, sent word to Tompkinson that when I got better he would be joining Robo in hospital.

To give him his due Tompkinson did not flinch or plead for mercy, instead he just laughed and sent word back that he would be waiting and when I turned up I would be the one joining Robo in hospital. I was fuming and the scene was set for a bust up between us.

Come my first day back you could feel the tension in the air even before I had got to school. All the kids turned to face me when they saw me coming and a few of them yelled out words of greetings.

"Hi Harry."

"How you doing Harry?"

"Glad you're back, Harry."

"Looking well Harry."

I didn't respond. I was too hyped up. So, instead, I just kept on walking and when people saw me coming they moved out of the way. Everybody that is except one dozy prat with glasses who just stood there gawping at me with a gormless expression on his face and didn't move even though it was obvious he was in my way. Still that wasn't a problem, as soon as I got close enough, I just pushed him out of the way and he flew through the air before hitting the deck. I wasn't fazed. I just stepped on his head and continued on.

Once at school, I was hoping to see this so-called hard kid from Liverpool in the playground because that is where most kids congregated before the bell rang, but he wasn't there. He wasn't anywhere else I looked either. So I shook my head and said to my crew, "Fuck it, I'll get him at break later on." It was annoying. But what else could I do?

Still, as it happened I would see him long before that. Every morning before class all the kids would head off to the main hall for morning assembly and once there I saw this red-haired kid, sitting a few lines down looking at me with a sneer on his face.

I turned to Winto. "Is that him? Is that the new kid who thinks he's cock of the school?"

"Yeah," said Winto. "It is."

I nodded, and then went storming forward shoving kids out of the way as I did. Whatever this prat had expected as he stood there with a sneer on his face it wasn't this, and before he knew it I had punched him so hard he had literally flown through the air and wound up in front of the stage.

I wasn't finished yet and yelled at everybody, teachers and kids alike to, "Get the fuck out of my way or I will do you too," before turning back to Tompkinson and yelling, "Fancy my crown do you? Think you're the cock of the school do you, well come on then, let's get to it."

Tompkinson, though, was in no position to fight back because he was already battered and bruised, and somewhat bog eyed, but I didn't let up. I continued to punch him in the face until he lay there, unconscious, and covered in blood. Then I let go of his head, letting it slump to the ground before throwing my hands in the air and yelling, "Awoooooooo," at the top of my voice.

For that I was hurled before the headmaster and suspended for a week. I think the headmaster wanted to expel me altogether, and I know Tompkinson's father pleaded with him to do so, but I wasn't expelled. I think it was because both of them received phone calls at home warning there would be dire consequences if I was.

So after my suspension was lifted, I returned to school and nobody questioned my right to call myself cock of the school after that, not that they had much time to do so if they wanted to.

A few weeks later, I left the school to make my way in the big bad world along with all the other fifth years. I had enjoyed my time there and I'm sure both staff and kids would remember me, though not necessarily for the right reasons.

Still, as I passed through the school gates for the last time I could not help but turn back and yell, "Awoooooooo," before turning around and getting on with the rest of my life. A life that would involve violence, more violence, and even more violence and I would love every moment of it.

HOOLIGAN

I left school and started to look round for a job. Both my brother and sister had gone to college and were now at university, but that was a non-starter for me. I just wasn't bright enough to enrol at college even if I had wanted to, which I didn't, so as I say it was a non-starter. Joining the army, navy or air force was also out of the question because that involved discipline and I didn't have any.

I did, for a moment, consider a career as a bricklayer but that involved manual work and I wasn't keen on that either.

I wound up working as a bouncer on the doors of a local pub called the Squire. Fighting was the one thing I was really good at, and at six foot two I really looked the part. I was also working at the roughest pub in Millwall, which was good news for management, because many of the regulars had gone to my school and knew of my fierce reputation. Word soon got around that Harry the Dog was manning the doors, and people would be very unwise to go there and take liberties.

I also became quite pally with the rest of the bouncers, many of whom were either black or of Irish origin. We'd get a takeaway after work and then go to somebody's house to watch a video and down some bevvies.

One night after work, I met up with the O'Conner brothers. They were in their early twenties and both showed promise as boxers. We had a curry at the local Indian but they couldn't come back and watch some videos as they were off to Ireland in the morning to visit their mother and wanted a good night's sleep.

As they made their way to their car they were confronted by a group of lads they had clashed with a couple of weeks earlier.

I saw what was happening and sneaked up behind them before yelling, "Awoooooooo," and storming into the lot of them, sending them fleeing for their lives (well apart from the three I had knocked out with my bare hands that is.)

That encounter sealed a bond of friendship with the O'Conner brothers which has lasted to this day. We'd shoot up to the West End every Wednesday to chill out and chat up the local girls. More importantly they had links to Millwall F.C.

As a kid I had found it far more fun to play football than to go anywhere and watch the local team playing at the Den. As a teenager me, Robo, and the rest of the gang had gone up there one Saturday to watch Millwall playing Liverpool, but the amount of racial abuse meted out to the black players by the crowd was disgusting and I had stormed out of the stadium in disgust.

The O'Conners though, were not exactly your average run of the mill fan. They were football hooligans, and every Saturday would meet up with fellow hooligans to fight each other up and down the country, often with knives and baseball bats, but usually with their boots and fists.

Because they only worked the doors Monday to Friday, as indeed did I, they had their weekends free, and had the time and money to pursue their hooligan activities. They would make their way to the Dog and Gun, a five-minute walk from the Den, wearing the latest fashion and tooled up with knives, hammers, and other weapons concealed in their jackets and wait for the rest of the firm, as football gangs called themselves, to turn up. Then they would head off to the game.

My first foray into the hooligan world took place inside the Dog and Gun. Millwall was playing Southampton at home and I told the O'Conner brothers I would meet them there along with the rest of my gang.

We were just walking up the road to the pub when I spotted some kid on a bike staring at me with an odd expression on his face. Then he ditched his bike and legged it into the pub. We carried on walking, and then all of a sudden I heard a lot of yelling and screaming and a gang of youths came storming out of the pub.

I thought they had come out to welcome us to the firm and let out a huge, "Awoooooooo" in mock salute, but as it turned out I was wrong.

The kid on the bike was what was known as a spotter, somebody who kept watch outside of a pub to stop a rival firm sneaking up and taking the occupants by surprise, and he had mistaken us for members of a rival firm. That could have been problematic, particularly as the O'Conner brothers had not yet arrived to vouch that we were Millwall and not their opponents. But as it happened, my *awhoooooooo* was quite infamous in Millwall, and it didn't take long for people to realise who I was and back off sheepishly as I brushed past them and entered the pub.

Next thing I knew was I was part of a merry group. All of them had heard of me and all of them wanted to be my friend.

"How you doing, Harry?"

"Pleased to meet you, Harry."

"Fancy a drink Harry?"

Then this hard-looking guy walked in and barged his way to the front. "Who the fuck are you?" he yelled putting his face up to mine.

I put my glass down and squared up to him. This guy was older than I was, and had an air of menace about him, but if he didn't back down, I would chin him and teach him a lesson he would never forget.

"That's Harry the Dog," cried one of the O'Conner brothers as they walked through the door. "It's OK, he's with us."

"I never asked you who he was," yelled the man rounding on him angrily. "I asked him."

He turned back to me and again put his face up to mine.

I was not the least bit fazed. Any minute now I was going to deck him. In fact I should have decked him already, but something was holding me back and I didn't know what it was, or did I? Well actually I did. It was because if I decked him, it would break the face off we were having, and I didn't want to do that. I just wanted to stare at him until he backed off and lost face in the process. Then I would deck him.

The tension in the pub was getting worse.

Even the barmaids and landlord were staring at us and in fact there was no longer a person in the pub that did not have their eyes on us.

The prat was feeling the heat too. His eyes were no longer cocky but apprehensive. He knew I was not going to back down, he could see it in my eyes, but he didn't know what to do about it. Normally he would just lash out with his fists when somebody faced up to him, as he had no doubt done in the past. But there was something about me that was telling him that would be a mistake, a very bad mistake, and so he did nothing as much as he wanted to.

Suddenly, the door burst open and the kid I had spotted earlier rushed in. "There's a mob heading this way," he yelled, "and I think they're Southampton's firm."

That did it. The man stopped staring at me and headed for the door. "Let's get the bastards," he yelled over his shoulder.

I smiled to myself. He was trying to make out that the reason he was walking away was because a rival firm had turned up and wanted to fight them, but I knew better. I had scared him and he didn't want to fight me. I saw it in his eyes.

Outside, the lads were yelling and screaming at the Southampton mob who were about forty strong, roughly the same number we had.

I pushed people out of the way as I made my way to the front. The prat stood there and it was obvious he was the leader of Millwall's firm by the way everybody was following him and standing behind him. I stood next to him and he glared at me angrily before looking away quickly and back at the Southampton mob. As I said, I frightened him.

Meanwhile, Southampton's mob were yelling and screaming, but doing nothing more, so I decided to take things in hand.

"Awoooooooo," I yelled, before dashing forward and steaming into the lot of them.

The Millwall lot were taken aback at first, but soon come steaming behind me and laying into our rivals and fights were breaking out everywhere. The prat was lashing out in all directions and putting up a good show. I saw him headbutt one guy and follow through with a kick in the balls. I also saw him pull out a hammer and smash it into the face of an oncoming skinhead. Most of my time however, was focussed on knocking out members of the rival firm.

I just knocked out one after another, either with my fists or boots. One geezer came up behind me and tried to put me in a headlock. I punched him so hard in the kidneys, that he yelped and loosened his grip instantly. I surged forward as if to take a rugby kick and then kicked him hard in the balls. He flew through the air and wound up on the ground yelping in even more pain. Then I turned to my left with my fists clenched.

I didn't know who was friend or foe. One hooligan looked very much like another to me. Then I heard the sound of police sirens and that was it, both mobs were running in opposite directions ... us to the pub, and them, to God knows where. The only people who did not run were those hooligans on both sides, who were either lying flat out on the pavement or were too injured or dazed to run.

Back in the pub I was buzzing. I had taken part in my first hooligan ruck, and enjoyed every moment of it. Robo and the rest of my gang were buzzing too. They had followed me into battle and come off best just as I had.

Then, the prat walked back into the pub and the place once again fell silent. Everybody was wondering if we were going to continue where we had left off. I was wondering that too, put my glass down, and fixed him with a firm stare.

It wasn't the same as before, however. I had seen him fighting and my respect for him had gone up. He had been there in the thick of it and put up a good show in the process. I think he sensed that my respect for him had gone up because his face softened and he came over with his hand outstretched.

"You fought well Harry," he said, his face breaking into a grin, "and you certainly live up to your reputation. Now I see why they call you Harry the Dog."

"So you know who I am," I said sarcastically. "Yet you asked me who I was earlier."

He glared at me and then noticing the slight twinkle in my eyes, his grim features lit up.

I asked him who he was.

"Bomber," he replied shaking my hand. "I lead this firm."

It wasn't long before I knew all of Milllwall's firm by name, and who were its key players. People like Ginger Bob for example, who started fighting with the firm when he was nine years old, believe it or not, and is a living legend in his own right. Booby the Wolf, so called, because he liked to gouge his opponents' eyes out with his claws, and eat their hearts; or so rumour had it. Mad Pat, who lived up to his name because he really was as 'mad as a hatter'. Winkle, or Wee Von Winkle as we called him because he liked to sleep a lot, and Higgsy who could make everybody laugh even when he was not trying to.

These were the main faces at Millwall at the time; or F-Troop as they were better known because hooligan firms liked to give themselves grand sounding names. I'm not going to say too much about them here, because they are all thinking about writing their own autobiographies, and you will be able to read about their exploits there.

I made a lot of other friends in those days too, such as Billy Plummer and a young lad called Gary Roberts. Both of them ran with F-Troop and now I was a member I used to come into the Squire a lot to relax and chill out for a while.

Indeed the Squire became a regular venue for F-Troop, which did not go down well at the Saxon down the road because that was popular with members of Chelsea's firm the Headhunters, and trouble was bound to follow. The only thing was it wasn't the Chelsea mob who started it but us.

We got fed up with these bozos drinking in a pub so close to our own, and reckoned they were doing it simply to take the piss, even though many of them lived in the area. We sent word that they were to piss off and find somewhere further away to drink, or the future would not be bright.

Instead of doing so, though, they issued threats of their own. Tempers flared and one night we burst into the Saxon and began laying into any of the Chelsea firm we could find.

That wasn't easy because as soon as we burst in the front door, most of them were scarpering out the back, but we gave chase and ran most of their mob up the road to Lower Sydenham station.

Hand to hand fighting quickly followed and fists were flying in both directions. I got a couple of good punches in and knocked two of them out instantly, but one of them sneaked up behind me and smacked me with a knuckleduster causing me to hit the ground seeing stars. By rights, I should have got up and kicked his scrawny head in, but I was too dazed to do anything but crawl aimlessly on the floor.

Luckily though, we had overwhelming numbers and it wasn't long before Chelsea's mob was legging it down the street, except for one poor soul who was caught by our lads and done over with a glass. His injuries could have been fatal that day, had he not been wearing one of those thick wrap cardigans, which were common in the seventies, and which deflected most of the blows as they stabbed him.

Not that we knew that at the time. We only found that out after we left him bloodied and bruised, and a well-known face called Little Tommy from Paddington told us about it later.

Alive or dead, the scene had been set. The word that we had attacked Chelsea in their own pub soon got out and it was obvious they would want revenge because they had lost face and in the hooligan world saving face is everything.

I too wanted revenge, particularly against the bastard who had knocked me for six with his knuckleduster. In fact knuckleduster man as I had labelled him was my number one target at that moment, so there were cheers all round when we heard our next home game was against Chelsea.

As usual we met in the Dog and Gun and had spotters out trying to locate the Chelsea Headhunters, which wasn't easy because this was the 1970s and back then there were no mobile phones.

Once one of our spotters spotted them getting off a coach, or more likely getting off a train down at the station, they had to relay word back to us, which meant using the public phone and that could be time-consuming if there was already a line of people waiting to use it. Still, word soon reached us that they were heading our way and we dashed out of the pub to meet them.

Outside, we walked down the street in the direction we were told they were coming from and it wasn't long before we spotted them. "Mill… Mill… Millwall," we screamed throwing our hands in the air.

"Chel… Chel… Chelsea," they yelled doing likewise.

For a few seconds there was silence as both groups eyed the other up and then without warning I yelled, "Awoooooooo," which caused the Chelsea mob to stare at me in surprise before I sprang forward and went steaming into the lot of them.

At first Chelsea were thrown into disarray and I heard somebody yell, "Who the fuck is that lunatic?"

But I wasn't listening. I was lashing out with my fists and boots in all directions, decking anyone and everyone who was getting in my way.

I wasn't on my own. Bomber, Winkle, and Ginger Bob were doing likewise and it seemed the fight was going our way, but until your opponents turn and flee or they are lying battered and bruised on the floor then you haven't won. The battle was still raging with fights going on everywhere. So, I continued to kick, punch, and headbutt one Chelsea Headhunter out of the way, followed by another.

It was brilliant and I was loving every moment of it, but it wasn't going all our way. Robo was on the floor wincing in agony, after a couple of Chelsea lads had laid into him with their boots and fists, and a couple of our lads were lying on the pavement out for the count.

Then I saw him, knuckleduster man I mean. He was wearing a green bomber jacket and attacking opponents from behind when their attention was engaged elsewhere, as he had done to me. What a coward.

Rage overcame me and without warning I puffed out my chest and threw my head back before yelling, "Awoooooooo."

That made me feel better but it scared the hell out of Chelsea, because they all froze and glared at me wondering what I was on. I wasn't fazed. I just lunged at knuckleduster man with such ferocity he wound up on the floor unconscious. I then took his knuckleduster and glanced at the sky before yelling "Awoooooooo," and throwing my hands up in victory.

This was too much for the Chelsea mob, who began backing off slowly before turning on their heels and legging it down the street, one guy yelling, "What lunatic asylum did they get him from?" in the process.

SHOTGUN

It didn't take long for Chelsea to discover that the thug with the strange howl was called Harry the Dog, because they sent word that the next time our teams met they were going to do me, and give me something to howl about... I had to laugh at that but as Millwall and Chelsea weren't due to meet again until the New Year, I just shook my head and got on with my life.

Soon I was following Millwall up and down the country and fighting rival firms in the process. First in Bolton, Blackpool, Cardiff, and Oldham, and then Wolverhampton, Carlisle, and Burnley. Of these Bolton was a pushover, Blackpool and Oldham even more so. Wolverhampton, Carlisle, and Burnley put up a decent fight and Cardiff because they had overwhelming numbers and were fighting on their home turf sent us fleeing for our lives.

I used to boast about these rucks at work, particularly to Linda who worked behind the bar. She was a pretty little thing and one night after work invited me home for sex.

Because it was near midnight when we got there, she told me to tread quietly as her parents were asleep upstairs and she didn't want to wake them. I too, didn't want to wake them given I was planning on making hay with their daughter, so I virtually tiptoed into the house and all went well until I got to the top of the stairs. Because Linda hadn't put the light on, through fear of waking her parents, I hadn't realised there was a large black cat dozing there and as I stepped on its tail, the little blighter hissed in anger before scurrying past me and sending me tumbling down the stairs, leaving me somewhat bog eyed at the bottom.

Linda's dad came bursting out of his bedroom door in his pyjamas with his wife standing sheepishly behind him and once they saw what had happened, they stood there smiling as Linda helped me to my feet. Linda's dad was Tommy Patterson, a long-distance lorry driver who worked down at the docks and delivered produce all round the country. He was away Monday to Friday, leaving his wife on her own, which was one of the reasons Linda had never left home despite being a grown woman in her thirties.

Over thirty or not, Linda was great in bed and taught me things about sex that would make a whore blush. In fact, Linda was the one who first introduced me to bondage. She liked nothing more than to handcuff me to the bed, gag me, and then have her wicked way with me after I had been subdued and rendered helpless.

After one bondage session, Linda removed the handcuff and the gag and was soon asleep beside me in the bed. It was half past two in the morning and I was dying for a leak but I didn't want to put the light on to get dressed, in case I woke her from her beauty sleep. So

I fumbled about in the dark until I found the door and crept out onto the landing. It was pitch black and it took me some time to find the bathroom, but eventually I did and found the light before closing the bathroom door behind me.

Coming out a minute or two later, I got the shock of my life. Linda's mum was standing there and I was about to yell in surprise when she clasped her hand over my mouth and said, "Don't say a word big boy, just come with me."

I was too shocked to say anything and she took me back to her bedroom before closing the door and having sex with me.

I ended up getting treated as a sex slave by both of them after that, with Linda never knowing that her mother had the hots for me too. So much so, that when both of them were killed in a car crash a few weeks later, while on their way to visit her grandparents in Devon for Christmas, along with their dad, I was devastated. I felt as though I had lost my two best friends.

To football hooligans I'm Harry the Dog, a man who fears nobody and will punch them to kingdom come when our paths meet. But to women I'm just an irresistible hunk, and they can't keep their hands off me.

I passed my driving test in the New Year and bought myself a brand new motor, a Ford Cortina, which I got from Fat Sammy's, a second-hand car dealer from Woolwich and a well-known face in the manor.

It was now 1977 – the era of punks, mods, and rockers. I wasn't particularly keen on any of them but I did like to strut my stuff on the dance floor, so there I was with Robo and the rest of my gang boogieing away in a club in the West End when up came this group of lads and one pushed me out of the way. To be frank, I was gobsmacked because he was such a weedy looking character; in fact, he had such a feminine look about him, that he looked like a poof. But whoever he was, he was bang out of order and I punched him so hard he flew through the air and ended up unconscious on the floor.

"Awoooooooo," I yelled before turning to his mates who were looking at me as though I had escaped from some mental asylum. My plan was to deck the lot of them but just then, two bouncers appeared out of nowhere and grabbed hold of me.

"Get your fucking hands off me now," I yelled, "or you'll end up like him."

They both glared at me angrily for a few seconds before one of them gasped and pulled away from me quickly.

"Whoa," he cried. "That's Harry the Dog, I remember him from school. A real hard bastard."

I glared at him. He may have remembered me but I didn't remember him. "Who the fuck are you?"

"Sammo," he said. "I was a few years above you at senior school. Don't you remember me?"

Well I didn't but I wasn't going to argue the toss about it. So I told him to chuck out the prat and his weedy mates before I lost my temper.

He gasped. "I can't do that Harry."

"Why not?" I growled.

"Because the guy you've just decked is Nigel Crane, Mickey Crane's brother," cried one of the weedy guys piping up with a grin on his face, "and when he finds you he will kill you."

I leaned forward and headbutted him so hard he hit the deck with blood gushing out of his nose. His mates backed off hastily and once again, I told the bouncers to throw them all out.

"But… but… we can't do that Harry," Sammo cried, looking as though he was about to burst into tears. "He's Mickey Crane's brother as I told you. The man's a psychopath."

I gave him a look. "If you're too fucking scared to throw some prick out because you're scared his brother will come after you, then you're in the wrong business."

He opened his mouth to protest but words failed him and I grabbed the prick off the floor and threw him head first out of the club. The others rushed past me and I told them to pick him up and piss off. I swear to God I've never seen a bunch of weeds dragging their mates down the road as quickly as they did.

That was on the Friday night and by rights I should have been working the doors down at the Squire, but the pub had sprung a water leak so the landlord had closed it until a plumber had fixed the problem. So the following morning when I met up with Millwall's crew in the Dog and Gun I was in high spirits after enjoying myself on the dance floor the night before.

To be honest though the day was nowhere near as exciting as we thought it would be. We were playing Nottingham Forrest at home and we were all hyped up because their firm the Forrest Executive Crew had a pretty, tasty reputation and one which deserved respect. But as so often happens on these occasions the whole thing was a washout because the police were on the ball that day and ensured that as soon as Forrest got off their train they were escorted up to the ground preventing us getting anywhere near them.

Gary (Boatsy) Clark in his book *Inside the Forrest Executive Crew* does not mention this encounter and I can't say I blame him because in the absence of neither of us getting anywhere near the other, both then and at the match, we were left with the only thing we could do, which was to hurl abuse at each other, while jumping up and down like prats and waving our fists in the process.

In fact, football hooliganism is a lot like that. Today, when you go into a bookstore and roam the shelves you will find endless books written by former hooligans like me telling you about their exploits and what they got up to with their respective firms back in the seventies and early eighties, some of which are good and others crap but all of them have one thing in common. They overplay the violence that is endemic in football hooliganism and play down the disappointments that come with it.

That is not surprising, as all hooligans write their autobiographies simply to make money and boast about what naughty boys they were, including me. So, the violence is overhyped, and the disappointments that come with it are downplayed; and trust me there are disappointments.

Travelling miles up and down the country for example to take on a rival firm only for them to put in a no-show is one of them, and for them to leg it the minute they spot you is another, but the worst is what happened that day. If a firm fails to show up or legs it the minute they spot you at least you can class that as a victory, and you can argue that they were too scared to fight. But when they turn up and you want to steam into them, but the police are blocking your way, that's another thing altogether and as I say, the day was a disappointment all around.

Mind you, that wasn't the only disappointment of the day. My mum was an excellent cook and usually had my tea ready for me when I got in about six o'clock, as I usually did when Millwall was playing at home, but she was in Wales with dad visiting her sister so I was at home alone.

My brother and sister were away at university by this time, so I could either make a sandwich, or ring up for a takeaway. Cooking myself a hot meal, was out of the question as I couldn't even boil an egg, and as I wanted something more substantial than a sandwich, that left a takeaway. So I rang up for a pizza and while I waited, had a hot shower and washed my hair as I was off clubbing down the West End later with Robo and the rest of the lads.

I had just dressed and was thinking what a handsome devil I was as I flicked my hair back in the mirror when the doorbell rang. Oh good, I thought, the pizza man's arrived. Bounding down the stairs, I opened the door expecting to see the usual guy from the pizza shop wearing his trademark crash helmet and holding my pizza in his hands.

Instead, I found this tough-looking skinhead glaring at me with hate in his eyes, and fists clenched. Next thing I knew he'd leapt forward and headbutted me so hard I hit the deck and was out for the count, with blood pouring down my face and clothes.

HOSPITAL

The first thing I knew about it was when I woke up in the back of an ambulance and found myself being driven at full speed through the streets of London towards the nearest hospital, but even then everything was a bit of a haze.

It was only when I got to the hospital and had been seen by the doctors that events started flooding back and when they did, I virtually leapt from the trolley and made a beeline for the door. My plan was to find out who had assaulted me and to put the bastard in intensive care for the rest of his miserable life, but a nurse blocked my way and told me that I was being taken up to the ward, and kept in overnight for observation.

"What the fuck for?" I cried, fixing her with a firm stare. "I'm fine now."

"Because you were suffering from concussion when you were brought in," she said coldly, obviously not liking my use of the f word, "so we need to keep you in for observation."

I didn't have a chance to object, because just then two police officers showed up and said they wanted a word. I wasn't expecting to see them because I hadn't reported the assault and hadn't expected the hospital to do so either, given the place was full of people who had suffered violence in one form or another and they hadn't called the police in about them.

However, as it turned out it wasn't the hospital who had called them. It was the pizza man after he had found me flat out on the doorstep and had rang for an ambulance. Still, the police didn't waste time.

"Harry Dog?" asked one, fixing me with a firm stare.

"Yeah," I spoke coldly.

"Mind if we have a word?"

Well to be honest it was a silly question because when the police ask if they can have a word, it usually means they're going to have one whether you like it or not, so I said, "What about?"

Well that was another silly question too because it was obvious what it was about. It was about the assault, so I told them I had no idea who it was who had assaulted me, or why, which was true, but then I went on to say whoever it was, was black. Well I had to say something to get them off my back and I didn't want to say anything that could lead them to my attacker before I could put him in intensive care. Saying they were black struck me as the best way to achieve this because the police would look for my attacker amongst the black community and leave me time to find the little runt and mete out punishment of my own.

The danger, of course, was that the pizza delivery boy may have seen my assailant and told them he was white, which meant I would have to think fast on my feet, but as it happens he hadn't, and the police noted my description and went on their way.

From then on, I was like a man on a mission. I may not have known my attacker's name, but I was convinced that he was either somebody I had chucked out of the pub, or he was a member of a rival hooligan firm. Of the two I was more inclined to think it was linked to football hooliganism. I have a pretty good memory for faces and never forget people who have given me grief at the door no matter how long it has been, so if I had encountered him at work I would have known about it and remembered him.

Football hooliganism on the other hand was another thing. As I've said before hooliganism attracts all sorts of headbangers and when two firms are laying into each other you don't always have time to remember a face, let alone know you have knocked them out, because you are too busy lashing out in all directions and trying to make sure you don't suffer the same fate. So, I could well believe that the person who had assaulted me was some thug I had knocked out during one of the football rucks I had been involved in and what's more I was pretty sure which firm the bastard belonged to – the Chelsea Headhunters.

Not only were the Headhunters our nearest rivals and ones I had had problems with before, as shown with that incident involving knuckleduster man, but the person who attacked me had spoken with a cockney accent and was a skinhead. In fact he looked like he was a member of the NF, with his denim jeans, green jacket and Dr Marten boots, and no football firm in the seventies had more links to the NF than the Chelsea Headhunters. In fact they still do today despite the protestations of some of its members.

So, I told the guys down at the pub that I was going to confront the Headhunters and get my hands on the little runt who had assaulted me and put him in intensive care, but Bomber threw a spanner in the works.

"I doubt it was them Harry because there is a golden rule amongst hooligan firms, that you never target anybody at home, no matter how much they hurt you when you meet, and the Chelsea Headhunters have never broken that rule, despite the rucks we have had over the years."

"You're joking?"

But, it turned out he wasn't. Football firms really do have an unwritten rule that you never attack anybody in their home, even if they have stabbed you when you fought them and even if you did wind up putting them in intensive care. The reason for this so-called act of chivalry, or so hooligans like to pretend, is to prevent innocent people getting hurt, particularly the elderly, women, and children, but don't be fooled. That's a load of old guff. The real reason is they don't want anybody turning up at their homes and attacking them or their families as they lay in bed. To prevent this they agreed not to attack people at home – and to pretend it is for the most magnanimous of reasons.

Still, I didn't give a damn about any so-called hooligan code of honour, I had my own code of honour to follow, and it was simply this, do unto others as they would do unto you. I found out where one of the Chelsea Headhunters lived and I went round to pay him a visit.

The man lived alone and his eyes nearly popped out of his head when he opened the door to find me standing there with a shotgun in my hand.

"Get the fuck inside," I yelled pushing him backwards and slamming the door behind us. "Now," I said as I placed my shotgun on his chin and forced his head upwards so he was staring at me. "Attack me at my home would you?"

"No… no Harry," he cried shivering like a drowned rat. "It wasn't us it was Mickey Crane."

"Mickey Crane? Who the fuck's he?"

"He's a right psychopath Harry, and attacked you over some ruck you had with his kid brother a couple of weeks back in a club up the West End."

I cast my mind back to the incident in question. So that was it. I had been assaulted because I had punched some jumped up little weed and not because of my hooligan activities or work on the doors.

I was fuming with myself for not realising that sooner. After all that prat on the door, Sammo, had warned me the man was a nutter and a man not to trifle with, but I never took it seriously and why should I? After all, I had worked the door for over a year now and it wasn't the first time I had punched some little weed in the face after he had tried to push his weight around, only to be told he was going to get his older brother on me, or some other toe rag he thought would scare me.

But this was the first time I had ever had somebody come to my house and confront me on my own doorstep. I was fuming, but now I knew who I was looking for, I could at least go looking for him and teach the little bastard a lesson he would never forget. So I pushed the gun further up the man's chin and said, "Address please."

"But I don't know where he lives Harry. I swear I don't."

I cocked the handle back.

"But… but I don't Harry," he yelled, bursting into tears. "I swear I don't."

"Then how do you know it was him who attacked me?" I demanded.

"Because he's NF Harry, and some of the Chelsea Headhunters are NF and they were talking about it in the pub."

"Were they?" I said curling my lips back into a grin, "and what were they saying?"

"They said he must have been fucking mad to take you on."

I glared at him. Either he was just saying that to please me or he was telling the truth, but whichever it was, it did the trick. I didn't blow his head off. Instead I told him that if he ever told anybody about this, I would be back to finish the job.

"Oh but I won't Harry," he blabbered. "I promise you I won't."

I stared at him for a few seconds before nodding my head and slamming the door shut on my way out.

MICKEY CRANE

It didn't take me long to find out more about Mickey Crane. Indeed, it turned out that the man was so infamous it was amazing that I had never heard of him before. Certainly, if you were involved with the NF in the mid 1970s, you would have heard about him and with good reason. He was the leader of the NF guard – a group of skinheads who comprised of some of the best street fighters on the neo-Nazi scene, and they were always punching, kicking, headbutting, and knocking out those who incurred their displeasure.

On one occasion, they had stormed into an Anti Nazi League (ANL) meeting in Walthamstow and smashed bottles into the faces of a group of 17-year-old girls who got in their way, while on another they had stormed a Jewish synagogue in North London and beat the residents with baseball bats before spraying swastikas all over the place.

Crane himself was in the thick of it. Most of the time he could be found at the front and laying into his opponents with such ferocity that he put some of them in intensive care and feeding off a drip for several months. On one occasion he stood next to the NF leader, John Tyndall and beat the crap out of any anti-fascist who tried to get near him.

In fact, the man was such an animal that he was not just feared by his opponents in the anti-fascist movement, but colleagues in the neo-Nazi movement as well and with good reason. Whenever neo-Nazis got together at a rally or music festival at home or abroad, Crane would take to the stage, cut the music, and announce that he would fight anyone there just to prove he was the hardest neo-Nazi around. Because of his fierce reputation nobody at home ever did, but that was not the case in Europe where other neo-Nazis were keen to show who was top dog.

This was clear at a Nazi festival in Sweden in June 1975 when after taking to the stage and throwing out his usual challenge, he found himself up against Ansgar Johansson, a Swedish neo-Nazi with a reputation for violence that rivalled Crane's.

Johansson had once led an attack on a refugee centre in Stockholm, smashing a bottle into the face of an African refugee and leaving the man severely wounded and blinded in one eye. On another occasion he had stamped on the head of an Arab shopkeeper after the man had asked for payment for some beer he had taken.

However, he was best known as leader of a racist bike gang called *H33*, the *H* representing Hitler and *33* meaning 1933 the year he came to power. Like Crane, he too had a reputation for throwing out challenges to all and sundry ... not just at Nazi meetings, but at bikers' festivals all round the country as was the case at a bikers' event at Gothenburg on the Swedish coast in November 1975.

At the event, Johansson had squared up to Axel Stumberg, a racist thug from a rival bikers' gang and the ensuing fight ended with Stumberg lying in a pool of blood, and Ansgar Johansson proclaiming himself the hardest man in the country.

As a result, when Crane and Johansson squared off, everybody was expecting a good scrap and they weren't disappointed.

It began with Crane moving forward and laying into Johansson with a volley of punches to the head, body, and face that sent him wheeling backwards and hitting the deck with considerable force, but it would take a lot more than that to put the big man out, and he was a big man. In fact he was six foot four and given Crane was only five foot ten it looked like David was fighting Goliath.

Nobody was surprised therefore, when Johansson got up and sprang at Crane with his arms outstretched. True, Crane ducked and hit the big man in the stomach causing him to gasp and crouch down in agony, but it was only for a second or two and before he knew it, Johansson had him by the throat and headbutted him with such force that Crane's eyes nearly popped out of his head and blood began gushing out of his nose.

How Crane recovered from that is anybody's guess, particularly as Johansson followed through with a kick to the head, which would have laid most men out, but somehow he did and was soon back on his feet and giving as good as he got.

Indeed, that was the thing about Crane. He may have been smaller than Johansson but by God that guy could take a punch and no matter how many times Johansson tore into him and smashed his huge fists into his gob, or the side of his head, and brought that huge head down on Crane's skull it was never enough. Even when Johansson give Crane one hell of a right hook that knocked him backwards, it still wasn't enough, and eventually the big man began to tire.

The notable thing about Crane was that he was a fitness fanatic and did not drink, smoke, or engage in any of the other vices most neo-Nazis engaged in. His favourite hobbies were fighting, Paki bashing and boxing down at his local gym, which made him supremely fit and able to take part in long bouts, unlike Johansson, I must add, who was not only overweight, smoked like a chimney and drank like a fish, but also took drugs.

As every second passed, and Johansson's movements and punches got slower and tiredness overtook him more and more, Crane was increasingly starting to get the better of him, and landing more and more punches to his head, body, and face.   Eventually, Johansson got to the stage where he could hardly throw a punch and was beginning to wobble. At this point, Crane then followed through with another flurry of punches to the head, body, and face, causing him to slump to his knees. Crane rushed forward and kicked him in the face, Johansson slumped to the floor, and that was it, the man was out for the count.

Impressive stuff wasn't it? The horde of boneheads cheering him on thought so, but I wasn't impressed by that, although now that I knew all about him it certainly explained why he had come to my house and attacked me on his own. I mean, he knew my name, he knew where I lived, and he must have known of my fierce reputation, but that hadn't stopped him confronting me on my own doorstep had it?   Given his prowess with his fists I could understand why he had been brave enough to confront me single-handedly, but it wasn't the end of the matter, because it was now me who wanted revenge and I was determined to get it.

I made my enquiries and found out that Crane really did live in Bermondsey, so I went round to pay him a visit, after getting his address from a contact at the local social security office. What was difficult however, was finding the place because everybody I stopped to ask directions to the house either could not speak English or didn't know where it was. Eventually, an old man pointed me in the right direction and it was about 9.30 at night when I pulled up outside his house.

To be honest, the area was nowhere as dodgy as I thought it would be. I was expecting to find myself on a rough council estate, with poor lighting, and youths on street corners. Instead, I found myself in a cosy little cul-de-sac, with large houses and well-kept gardens and as I said, it surprised me.

Still, I wasn't there to admire the scenery but to teach a little runt a lesson he would not forget. Wearing a large overcoat which concealed the shotgun I was carrying, I went round and knocked on his door.

The man himself did not answer but his kid brother did and when he clapped eyes on me, his eyes nearly popped out of his head.

"Fuck me," he cried. "What do you want?"

I headbutted him and he fell backwards and hit the floor.

I strode into the house and slammed the door behind me. "Now you little runt," I cried pulling the shotgun out and holding it up to his face, "let's find your brother so I can blow his fucking head off."

The little runt gasped and I yelled, "Mickey Crane. Come out to play."

There was no answer.

"Mickey Crane come out to play," I yelled again.

Still no answer.

"Listen you Nazi bastard," I yelled, "come out to face me if you've got the guts."

"But he's not here Harry," his brother yelled, eyeing the shotgun and shaking like a leaf. "He's not here."

"Oh aye," I cried, not believing a word he said. "Well let's see."

I frogmarched him from room to room looking under the beds, behind the couches, and in the wardrobes to see where he was lurking. But the little runt was right, he wasn't here.

"So where the fuck is he?" I cried pushing the shotgun further into his chin and raising his face so he was staring into mine. " Don't lie or I'll blow your fucking head off."

"He's in prison," he blabbered. "Maidstone prison."

"Maidstone prison," I cried surprised. "What the fuck's he doing in Maidstone prison?"

"Assault, Harry. He got six months for assaulting a black family at a bus stop outside Liverpool Street station last November. His trial was last week and he's been in prison since Friday."

"Has he?" I said dubiously.

"But… but... I can prove it Harry," he said desperately. "It's in the paper. I'll show you."

He walked into his sitting room and handed me a copy of the Bermondsey News and it was clear the weasel was telling the truth, because it was all over the front page. That was annoying because I had really been looking forward to giving Crane his just deserts.

Still it wasn't all bad news. "Listen you little prick," I said, once again shoving the shotgun up his chin and curling my lips back into a grin. "All this started because of you and because you wanted to play the hard man when you're nothing but a wimp who hides behind your brother's coat-tails. Well now I'm going to teach you a lesson and I mean a lesson and if you squeal on me to the police I'll be back to blow your fucking head off, got it?"

He was too scared to reply, and I tore into him with such ferocity that by the time I had finished he was flat out and lying in a pool of blood.

"Awoooooooo," I cried as I left the house and banged the door shut behind me. "Awoooooooo," I cried as I started the car and drove off into the night.

ARREST

The next day I was in bed when I heard banging on the door. Leaning out of the window I saw hordes of police officers, most of whom were clutching guns, running around like headless chickens. One of them spotted me and yelled out, "There he is now sir."

Then this older bloke with a moustache appeared and said, "Harry Dog?"

"Yeah,"

"Mind if I have a word?"

I smiled. "If I said no, would you piss off and leave me alone?"

His expression changed. "Downstairs now Dog," he growled.

"Not before I've put some clothes on," I said grinning and closing the window behind me.

When I got downstairs, I opened the door and was immediately pinned against the wall with police officers pointing guns to my head.

"Harry Dog," the guy with the moustache said. "I'm Detective Inspector Henshaw and I'm arresting you on suspicion of attempted murder."

"Attempted murder," I cried. "Who the fuck am I supposed to have attempted to murder?"

"Nigel Crane," he replied with a wry smile; "and I must warn you that you don't have to say anything but anything you do say will be taken down and may be used in evidence against you."

I opened my mouth to speak but another voice cut through the air.

"Don't say another word Harry, until you have received legal advice."

I glanced round and saw an elderly man in a shabby overcoat walking up the path with a stern expression.

"Who the devil are you?" cried Henshaw angrily, "and how did you get past my officers at the gate?"

The man flashed some identification. "I'm Mr Wilcox of Wilcox and Son's solicitors and I'm here to represent my client, Mr Dog on the charge of attempted murder I think I heard you say."

"You got here very quickly," cried Henshaw incredulously.

The man in the shabby coat coughed politely. "Not really officer. I only live up the road and after you had informed Mr Dog that you would like a word with him, he had the good sense to call me before opening the door to you."

Henshaw glanced at me coldly and I smiled at him in amusement. Didn't expect that you bastard did you, I thought to myself.

Down at the local police station I was taken to a small room and questioned by Henshaw with an officer sitting next to him making notes. With my solicitor sitting in a chair beside me the interview began.

I was asked if I knew a Nigel Crane and I said, "No." I was asked if I had turned up at his house with a shotgun the previous night and I said, "No," and I was asked if I owned a shotgun and I said, "No."

He then asked where I had been the previous night at around 9 p.m., to which I replied, "At home in bed because I had a headache and was not felling well."

"Oh yes," said Henshaw with a sceptical expression. "Any witnesses?"

"You mean like was I in bed with your wife?" I said with a grin.

Henshaw went red and I shook my head. "No there are no witnesses. I was home alone, as my parents are away in Devon."

"Oh what a surprise," said Henshaw sarcastically.

"You think so?"

My solicitor decided to intervene. "May I ask what evidence you have for suspecting my client of this crime Inspector? So far I have seen none."

Henshaw shifted uncomfortably in his chair. "Late last night the parents of Nigel Crane returned home from a night out and found their son lying in a pool of blood in the hallway. They rang for an ambulance and then notified the police. When questioned, Mr Crane informed them that he had been assaulted by Mr Dog here."

"Rubbish," I cried.

"For what reason would my client wish to harm Mr Crane?" enquired my solicitor sternly.

Again Henshaw shifted slightly in his chair. "Because according to Mr Crane, they had an altercation in a nightclub last month, which resulted in Mr Crane's older brother Mickey, going round and assaulting Mr Dog on his doorstep." He looked at me with a grin when he said that.

Once again my solicitor intervened. "You say Mr Crane was found lying in a pool of blood in his parents' house … may I ask where that is?"

"Bermondsey."

"Bermondsey," I cried incredulously. "Never been to Bermondsey in my life and as for this Mickey Crane … so that's the name of the black bastard who turned up on my doorstep and took me by surprise is it?"

Henshaw glanced at his colleague and then back at me in surprise. "Mickey Crane isn't black Harry. He's as white as you and me."

"Then he wasn't the bastard who turned up on my doorstep and assaulted me was he?" I growled. "That guy was as black as the ace of spades."

Henshaw stared at me.

"Check your records if you don't believe me, because I made a statement saying as much at the time."

He continued to stare at me before leaving the room with his colleague and saying he would be back shortly.

I watched them go and then turned to my solicitor who smiled and said, "Well done Harry you've got them on the run."

I had too, as was clear when Henshaw and his colleague returned because it turned out they had nothing to link me to the crime, no fingerprints, no blood spatters, nothing.

I wasn't surprised about that as I had travelled to Bermondsey in a stolen car and returned it without the elderly couple who owned it knowing it had been stolen, so there would be no blood in my car linking me to the crime. There would be nothing on any of the clothes I had worn either, because I had put them in a big bag and placed them in the old couples' bin knowing it was collection day and the binmen would be emptying the trash. In fact I had actually seen the binmen throwing the bag into the back of their dustcart as the police drove me to the station and I had laughed to myself when I did.

The police hadn't found a shotgun when they searched my house either, but that was hardly surprising was it? I was hardly likely to leave it at home in case Crane went squealing to the police and the latter came knocking on my door.

So, I was never charged with any offence and left the station a free and happy man and thinking what a silly boy Nigel Crane was for grassing me up to the police when I warned him not to. A very silly boy indeed.

HULL CITY PSYCHOS

Down at the pub it seemed the whole world and his wife knew that I had been arrested and taken down to the police station, which was hardly surprising given the police had turned up at my house clutching guns, banging away on my door, and waking the whole neighbourhood up in the process.

However, they were gobsmacked when I told them that I had been arrested on suspicion of attempted murder, because for some reason they thought it was to do with my football hooligan activities.

"So who the fuck are you supposed to have attempted to murder, Harry?" asked one F-Troop member nervously, "and why?"

"An annoying little runt called Nigel Crane," I replied reaching for my beer.

"Nigel Crane," he barked. "Who the fuck is Nigel Crane?"

"He's a fucking little weed who was stupid enough to have a dig at me in some nightclub the other week," I growled, "so I chinned him."

I took a swig of my beer and put my glass down. "But don't look at me like that guys. Whoever turned up at his house and put him in hospital, it sure as hell wasn't me. I was in bed at the time with a headache. So the little weasel must have pissed somebody else off."

I took another sip of my beer and glanced at Bomber. "And what the fuck's the matter with you? You look as white as a ghost."

"Did you just say Nigel Crane, Harry?" he asked nervously.

I nodded.

"He's not from Bermondsey is he and has a brother called Mickey?"

I nodded again. "So the police said."

"Fuck me," he cried. "Mickey Crane's one of the hardest men in the country. He'll stop at nothing to put the person responsible in hospital, that is if he doesn't kill him first."

I laughed. "Well he'll have to be quick about it, because the person who assaulted his brother turned up with a shotgun saying they were going to blow his fucking head off."

There were gasps all round and Bomber reached for his beer glass and said, "Bloody hell, there are some right fucking nutters about, some right fucking nutters."

"There are indeed," I cried reaching for my beer glass, "some right fucking nutters."

The following Saturday, Millwall were playing Hull City away which in hooligan terms meant F-Troop would be up against the Hull Psychos and I was really looking forward to it, because the last few days had been tense and I could really do with a good punch up to unwind and get things off my chest. The only problem was Hull was over two hundred miles away, which meant in order to arrive there before the game, we had to set off at five o'clock in the morning, and given I had only finished work at midnight meant little sleep.

So I trooped onto the coach bleary eyed and sat down as the driver pulled away and we began our long trip to Hull. Some of the lads were buzzing and saying what they were going to do to the Hull Psychos when they ran into them, but I was still knackered and could do with some kip so I put my head against the window hoping to get a good few hours' sleep. But, it was a waste of time because as is common on such occasions, beer was plentiful and by the time the coach reached the M1, I was swigging beer with the rest of the lads and having a merry old time in the process.

Once we got to Hull, we did what most firms do when they are on enemy turf so to speak. We went for a walk hoping to run into the enemy so we could kick their faces in and show them who was top dog, but that was easier said than done. The fact of the matter was we were in a strange town and did not know where the opposition was or what they looked like. For all we knew anybody coming towards us, any group of lads drinking in a pub, any motley crew lurking on a street corner could be the opposition and we had to be on our guard.

We didn't find them and in the end I said, "Fuck it, let's go and have a drink."

So, we went into some boozer and I was just thinking that the Hull Psychos should be called the Hull Pansies, when suddenly one of the guys I had told to stand outside the pub and keep an eye out in case they burst into the place and took us all by surprise, came running in and saying there was a bunch of tough-looking lads heading our way.

"Oh good," I cried, putting my beer glass down and storming out of the pub with the rest of F-Troop in tow.

Outside, I saw about thirty rough looking geezers coming towards us and I knew they were the Hull Psychos without them saying a word. I can't explain it, I just did, and before any of them could react I just threw my head back and yelled, "Awoooooooo," before dashing over and laying into them.

With me headbutting, punching, and kicking any of the Hull firm who got in my way, it wasn't long before they started to back off, but as they did I heard one of them say, "Who the fuck is that lunatic with the dark jacket, has he escaped from Rampton or what?"

"I'm Harry the Dog you prick," I yelled, "and don't you forget it. I'm the hardest hooligan there is."

With that I threw my hands in the air and yelled, "Awoooooooo."

The rest of F-Troop who had joined me in battle did likewise, and within seconds we were jumping up and down and toasting our victory. However, that wasn't the end of the matter.

Somebody must have phoned the police and told them there were gangs of lads fighting each other in the street, because the sound of police sirens suddenly filled the air and I turned to the rest of the firm and said, "Quick lads let's get away from here."

I dashed down an alleyway hoping it would bring us out on the other side of town, but it only lead to a dead end and even worse the police sirens were getting louder.

I knew if somebody had seen us running down the alleyway and told the police we would be trapped, because there was nowhere to hide, but thankfully nobody did and after a couple of police cars had driven past and their sirens had faded into the distance, I virtually tiptoed back to the entrance and peeped out to see if there were any police lurking about.

There weren't any. Well none that I could see anyway, although I could still hear the faint rumble of a police siren but that was getting fainter and fainter until at last it faded away altogether.

I stepped out onto the street with the rest of the firm following me and that was a mistake, because as soon as I did, two police officers walked round the corner and stopped a few feet from us. I was taken aback and my first thought was to chin them and leg it, but then common sense won the day and I tried to bluff it out.

"Do you know the way to Hull football ground?" I asked politely, fixing them with a polite smile.

"Certainly sir," one of the police officers replied, but before he could tell us, a police van came to a screeching halt beside us and out jumped some power-crazed sergeant who yelled at us.

"You lot up against the wall now."

"Why?" I yelled "For what reason?"

A bunch of police officers jumped out behind him and pushed us against the wall much to my fury and once again I wanted to chin a police officer but that would have been stupid. They had the full weight of the law behind them and I knew if I did that I would have been carted off down the nick and hauled before the magistrates in no time. So I just shook my head in disbelief and again asked why we were being pushed against the wall.

"Why?" he yelled pushing his face against mine. "Because you've been brawling in the street with some of the locals haven't you?"

"Are you mad," I snapped. "We've only just got here, and we were asking these two officers the way to the ground, weren't we officer?"

I fixed the one I had spoken to with a firm stare, and reluctantly he nodded his head. "Quite right Sergeant he was."

The sergeant was a right Hitler and clearly didn't like somebody getting the better of him. "Well I don't believe you," he bawled. "I think you're football hooligans who have come here to make trouble."

"Careful, Sergeant," I said politely. "That's slander."

He stepped forward and fixed me with a menacing stare. "Oh is it?" he said sarcastically. "Fancy yourself as a lawyer, do you?"

"I am a lawyer," I replied calmly, "a Queen's Counsel to be exact."

The expression on his face changed and the rest of the lads were pissing themselves laughing. But for some reason the bozo bought it and allowed us to go on our way, particularly when I told him that if he continued to detain us without any legal cause I would sue him for false arrest and I would be calling on the hordes of shop goers who were looking on as witnesses.

At Boothferry Park where Hull played their home games we piled into the stadium and took our place along with the rest of the Millwall fans.

In those days, most stadiums did not have seats and you had to watch the game standing up. I wasn't bothered about that or the fact that the Hull Psychos had suddenly reappeared and were giving it the big one knowing we couldn't do anything about it as they were on the opposite side of the ground and there were hordes of police officers between them and us.

What did piss me off though; was that one of the Millwall fans was doing his nut because Hull had a black player on their team and he was jumping up and down making monkey noises and calling him all the names under the sun.

"You dozy black bastard," he yelled, whenever the man got hold of the ball. "Or why don't you piss off back to ape land and take all those dirty niggers with you?"

In the end Robo went over and headbutted the man who fell back and hit the ground with blood pouring out of his nose. I thought the geezer would get up and fight back because he was quite a big man but he didn't. He just stared at Robo with a look of submission on his face, and it was obvious that despite his bluff and bluster the man was nothing but a coward. However, Robo wasn't finished with him yet.

"Apologise now," he growled.

The man just stared at him blankly.

"I said, fucking apologise now." Robo grabbed the man by the throat and pulled him to his feet.

The man just stared at him blankly again.

Robo went to strike him.

"I'm sorry, I'm sorry," the man cried and put his arms up defensively.

"Don't just apologise to me," yelled Robo, "but to him."

He pointed to the black player who was looking on with a look of incredulity on his face, as indeed was everybody else.

The man yelled, "I'm sorry."

"Louder," cried Robo.

"I'm sorry," yelled the man again.

"Louder," cried Robo.

"I'm sorry," yelled the man.

"Louder," said Robo.

"I'm sorry," screamed the man, so loudly that the stadium went quiet and everybody was looking and wondering what was going on.

Robo nodded.

On the coach back to Millwall, the beer was flowing and Robo was the hero of the hour but I wasn't celebrating with them. I was shattered, so lay on the back seat, and got some shut-eye.

By the time we got to Millwall in the early hours, I felt better, in good spirits and looking forward to our next ruck. Really looking forward to it in fact.

BLACKPOOL'S RAMMY ARMS CREW

The following week we were playing Blackpool at home and the minute they turned up at the train station our scouts alerted us to their presence and we dashed over to confront them, but it was a waste of time. The police had surrounded them and the best we could do was to follow them up to the ground, trading insults with them as we went.

Once there, we continued to swap insults until the game began and then settled down to watch it.

It had barely began when a voice yelled, "You fucking coon. You should have been put down at birth."

I wheeled round in surprise along with the rest of F-Troop.

The fat bozo from last week was just standing there with a smirk on his face and looking at us as though daring us to make something of it. I was surprised by his cocky attitude because of the cowardly way he had reacted after Robo had decked him last week.

Before I could do anything, I heard Robo say, "I don't fucking believe this", before going over to confront the man.

But something was wrong. I could feel it. The only way that big fat weasel would have the guts to do what he had was if he had back up. I yelled over to Robo, "Hold on mate it's a trap."

It was too late. The man stepped to one side and some hard-looking geezer stepped forward and eyeballed Robo.

"So you're the fucking coon who had a dig at my uncle last week are you?"

As he said this, a group of other hard-looking geezers who had been watching the game turned, surrounded Robo, and he was trapped.

"I said are you the fucking coon who punched my uncle last week?"

"He certainly is," I said pushing two of the goons out of the way and headbutting his uncle in the process.

The hard-looking geezer was aghast and took a swing at me, but I ducked it and punched him. He wound up on the ground next to his uncle with blood gushing out of his nose. I thought he would fight back but he didn't. Instead he just got up, gave me a cold look, and stormed off taking the rest of the prats he was with along with him.

I had to laugh at that because there is nothing funnier than a bunch of wimps being put in their place and then walking away with their tails between their legs, but it wasn't over yet. As soon as the game was over, the hard-looking geezer and his mates were back and the man challenged me to a one-on-one.

"A one-on-one," I said with a grin. "Not a problem."

I stepped forward to chin him but he put his hands out. "No no, not here. We're squaddies, and if we're arrested for fighting we could get kicked out of the army."

"Squaddies," I replied. "What regiment?"

"Parachute regiment," he barked.

"Fucking hell," Robo cried, "they're paras."

Some members of F-Troop shifted uncomfortably on their feet, but I wasn't impressed.

"Paras," I cried. "Look like wankers to me."

The hard-looking geezer glared at me angrily, as did his mates, but I didn't chin him there and then. The man had challenged me to a one-on-one and there was no way I was going to let it pass, not only because I would have lost face in front of the rest of the lads and that would never do, but more importantly I would have lost any self-respect I had, and that was never going to happen.

"If you don't want the one-on-one here, where do you want it?"

He grinned and replied, "Somewhere nice and quiet where we won't be disturbed."

"Lovely ... I know just the place."

We all trooped across the road and down some alleyway, but Bomber who had been looking on with some alarm, suddenly came to a standstill.

"Hold on Harry this could be a trap. These guys' mates could be lying in wait for us."

"You mean, like Mickey Crane and his Nazi buddies," I replied with a grin.

"Mickey Crane," cried the hard-looking squaddie. "You know Mickey Crane?"

"Not personally," I replied with a smile. "But I intend to make his acquaintance when he comes out of prison."

"Fuck me," cried one of his mates who had been staring at me with wide eyes, "you're not Harry the Dog are you?"

"Yeah. What of it?"

"Fuck me. You're not the guy who turned up at his house the other week intending to blow his head off with a shotgun but he wasn't there, so you put his brother in intensive care instead?"

I smiled. "What of it?"

Well the look on his face was comical, as indeed were the looks on all their faces and you could see they were having doubts about the wisdom of taking me on. Even their leader was looking worried, but don't be fooled. These guys were no cowards. There were about eighty of us, and thirty of them, but they were still following us down the alleyway so their top guy and I could have a one-on-one. As they were paras they could no doubt handle themselves.

However, before the fight could begin I heard a commotion behind us and I spun round thinking to myself, Christ have they led us into a trap after all because there were hordes of lads clutching bottles and yelling insults at us. But it soon became clear that they hadn't, because they were looking just as gobsmacked as we were.

The guys yelling abuse were wearing orange scarves and hats. I realised they were Blackpool's firm the Rammy Arms Crew, because they asked if we were Millwall's F-Troop and when we said yes, they came charging at us with everything they had.

I was taken aback and to this day I don't know if they had followed us from the stadium or just come upon us by chance, but right then that was the least of our problems. Right then Blackpool's mob was charging right at us. Before we could move forward to attack them though, we had to duck because they suddenly began tossing bottles through the air. Although I wasn't hit, one or two of the other lads were and they hit the ground with blood gushing out of their heads.

As soon as the barrage was over, I threw my head upwards and yelled, "Awoooooooo," before jumping into the hordes of thugs who were nearly upon us.

For the next ten minutes, fists were flying in all directions and I was lashing out at anybody wearing an orange scarf ensuring that they either hit the deck or backed away looking somewhat bog eyed as they did.

To give Blackpool their due, they were a tasty little outfit and certainly put up a better performance than the Chelsea Headhunters or other so-called top firms we had come across. However, as I said before we were playing at home and had the numbers and it wasn't long before Blackpool were on the retreat. In fact it wasn't long before they started to leg it, taking their injured friends with them.

On such occasions we would normally have given chase before giving them another hiding, but this time we didn't. Fighting can zap your energy and we all needed to catch our breath. So I just leaned against the wall with my hands on my knees waiting until I had fully recovered my strength and when I did, I threw my head in the air again and yelled, "Awoooooooo," to celebrate another victory over a rival firm.

Then I remembered why I was here and looked around for the squaddie hoping to have a one-on-one but the man was nowhere to be seen. Neither were any of his mates and it was obvious they had scarpered when my attention had been focussed elsewhere, but I can't say I blame them. I mean would you want to fight somebody who had turned up at a man's house with a shotgun and threatened to blow his head off? Those paras didn't and I never saw or heard from any of them again.

I never saw or heard from that fat sod either, which is just as well because if I had, he would have wound up in intensive care as Nigel Crane had done before him. Such was the fate that befell those who pissed off Harry the Dog.

THE PRATS FROM THE COUNCIL

By March 1977, my whole life revolved around football hooliganism and working the doors at the Squire. Most of the time things went smoothly down at the pub because most people knew of my fierce reputation and weren't too keen to cross me. The same could not be said of the prats down at the local council however.

I was on the door one night chatting away to the O'Conner brothers when I heard a commotion inside and dashed in to find this well-dressed woman yelling and screaming and clearly the worse for drink.

"What's going on?"

"She's had too much to drink, Harry," cried the landlord, "and she threw an empty glass at me when I refused to serve her more."

That was it; I grabbed her by the scruff of the neck and threw her head first out of the door where she wound up on the floor looking somewhat confused.

Sounds harsh I know, but as anybody who has ever worked the door will tell you, once somebody has started smashing the place up, there's little you can do but throw them out. When people are that rowdy what else can you do? But, the funny thing is that once you have dished out a bit of violence of your own and shown these bozos you will stand up to them, it's amazing how quickly they sober up.

This woman certainly did because she picked herself up off the ground and stormed off down the street, but not before turning around and yelling I would be sorry as she worked for the council and I was in big trouble.

That was on the Thursday and by the following week it had all but slipped from my mind, particularly given we had played Cardiff City at home that weekend and given their firm, the Soul Crew, a good hiding in the process.

However, the landlord of the Squire took me aside when I turned up for work on the following Wednesday and said somewhat nervously, "I'm sorry Harry, but there's no easy way to say this … I'm going to have to let you go."

"What," I cried. "Why?"

Again he shifted nervously on his feet. "Well Mr Grimes from the council said if I don't sack you, I will lose my licence to run the pub and the place would have to shut."

"Who the fuck is Mr Grimes?"

"He's the bigwig in charge of overseeing licences down at the council and making sure the licensee laws are followed."

"He is, is he? And why is he so keen for you to sack me?"

"He said it was because you threw his female colleague out of the pub last week and the council take care of their own!"

I stared at him in astonishment. I remembered the incident and the bitch saying she worked for the council and I was in big trouble, but never in my wildest dreams did I think she was serious. After all why should I? Drunks often made threats which they rarely carried out when they sobered up, everyone knew that. But this one had and now I was being laid off for simply doing my job ... well I wasn't having it.

I told the landlord he had two choices. Either he kept me on or I would get one of the local low lifes to burn his pub down and he would be out of a job too.

"But... but, I can't keep you on Harry," he pleaded. "If I do I'll lose my licence. Mr Grimes made that perfectly clear."

"Don't worry about Grimes, I'll deal with him. Meantime you are going to put me on paid leave."

"Paid leave?" he said surprised.

I nodded. "That way, you can tell Grimes you've sacked me while keeping me on the payroll at the same time."

"But... but I can't pay you for doing nothing."

"But you won't be," I said. "You'll be paying me to ensure none of the local low lifes burn your pub down while I'm busy dealing with Grimes won't you?"

Well he reluctantly accepted it and the next day I found out that Grimes lived over Acton way and was married to a very senior officer at Scotland Yard, which was annoying as there was no way I could go round to his house and have a word in his ear without incurring the wrath of Scotland Yard which I was not prepared to do.

It was also annoying that I could not find out who that drunken bitch was, because there is nothing I would have liked more than have a word in her ear too. In fact I was so bloody annoyed about it that the following weekend, I took my frustration out on the Bristol Gas Squad when we played Bristol Rovers away that Saturday.

What happened was the ref had just blown the whistle for half time when the Bristol mob began giving us the big one and calling us all the names under the sun; thinking they were safe, because they were on the opposite side of the ground and there were hordes of police officers between them and us. Normally they would be, but not today. Today, I was so pent up with fury that before I knew it I had stormed across the pitch, before leaping the barrier and laying into the Bristol Gas Squad with my fists and boots.

The Bristol mob were aghast and some of them began backing away anxiously, while others did a runner. The rest were either kicked, punched, or headbutted out of the way, but before I could do more, however, I was grabbed by police officers and bundled out of the ground yelling and screaming as I went.

Quite why I wasn't arrested and taken down to the police station and charged with a public order offence is anybody's guess, but this was the 1970s, and back then things were often done differently than they are today.

I wasn't complaining, but that still left the problem of how to deal with Grimes.

Over the next few days I followed him home from work, trying to work out some way of getting to him. I knew what he looked like because I got the landlord to point him out to me one morning when he arrived for work. I knew he was a fifty-year-old moron, who was as bald as a coot, and vastly overweight, but as I said before, violence was out of the question, because he was married to a senior police officer. I toyed with the idea of planting heroin in his car and then ringing customs and exercise and telling them where they could find it, but as it happened luck came to my rescue.

I was just following the bastard home on the following Tuesday, when to my surprise he turned left at the traffic lights next to Stanley Street and not right and I thought oh aye where are you going? Well it didn't take me long to find out he was heading over to Battersea, because I soon found myself on the A3205. I was just thinking what business have you got over there when to my surprise he turned off and pulled into a large building with a large sign saying the Motty Arms in front of it.

My eyes nearly popped out of my head when I saw that, because although I had never been there, I knew all about the Motty Arms. Back in the seventies it was quite infamous as a knocking shop and was the perfect place for people to have sex with someone they were knocking off, usually a colleague from work.

As soon as Grimes got out of the car a girl came running over to him and began kissing him passionately on the lips, and my eyes nearly popped out of my head when I saw who it was, for it was none other than the bitch who had boasted she worked for the council and was going to cost me my job.

Luckily, I had my camera with me. After I had planted heroin in his car and called customs, I had been hoping to take a picture of him getting arrested, so I could send it to the press and he would lose his job. So I started snapping away with my camera as she continued to kiss him passionately on the lips before they both let themselves into a room.

It was fantastic stuff and even better when I heard him say to the bitch, "I love coming here every Tuesday just to see you because it really makes my day."

It made my day too, because now there was no need to plant heroin in his car. I had pictures I could blackmail him with, but I needed time to get the pictures developed.

The following Tuesday I was back and once the lovers had gone into the room I gave them five minutes to undress and get into bed before I burst in.

"Who the hell are you?" cried Grimes, who was hiding under the sheets.

"It's the guy who threw me out of the pub the other week," replied the girl.

"It certainly is," I snapped. "And you're the bitch who went crying to your boss here, and told him to withdraw the pub licence if my boss did not sack me."

Grimes began blabbering and begging me not to hurt him but I said, "Shut it and listen up."

I told him that he was to ring my employer and tell him his licence was safe and he was to keep me on. I said if he didn't, I would send all of the pictures I had of him kissing his lover to his wife and the press. I took them out of an envelope and showed him the pictures in question.

He began blabbering again but I just punched him in the stomach. As he crouched down in agony, I took his wallet out of his trousers, which were hanging lamely over a chair, and took out all of his cash – £182 in total. I told him that all this had cost me time and money and it was only right he paid for it. I then told him to get dressed and piss off, which he did before driving away at considerable speed.

Then I got undressed and climbed into bed besides the girl. You may call it rape if you like, but this girl had tried to screw me out of a job. It was only right I screwed her in return.

BLACKBURN ROVERS

You would have thought the minute I had my wicked way with her and then drove off, she would have reported me for rape wouldn't you, but she didn't as I knew she wouldn't. It wasn't because of the way she looked at me when I took my clothes off and got into bed with her, that convinced me she wasn't going to go running to the police, but the way she got on top of me and took the lead after I did.

Any further proof however, came on Monday night when she turned up at the pub in a short skirt and told me my job was safe and the pub would not be losing its licence.

In reality she didn't need to tell me as the landlord had already phoned me and told me it was safe, but don't be fooled. That was not why she was here. She wasn't here to tell me my job was safe, but because she wanted my body again, which was perfectly understandable. I was quite a handsome dude and girls were always lusting after it, which was why she was wearing a short skirt and looking at me with puppy-dog eyes. So I duly obliged by taking her behind the pub and giving her a right good seeing to.

That said the girl was a weirdo by anybody's standards and trust me being a football hooligan I knew a lot of weirdos. Her name was Jackie Rylie and she worked for the council as a typist in the housing department, and how she managed to hold down a job in the council given her erratic behaviour was anybody's guess.

However, I guess the fact she was screwing Grimes had something to do with it as he was a council bigwig and held a hell of a lot of sway down there.

But how weird she was soon became clear the following night. She turned up again while I was working the doors and asked me to take her behind the pub and smack her backside.

"I beg your pardon," I said, thinking I had not heard her right.

"I said, I want you to take me behind the pub and smack my backside," she said looking up at me with those puppy-dog eyes again. "Do you think you are up for it?"

Well I have to admit it was the strangest request I had ever had in my life, but I duly obliged, much to the amusement of the other doormen.

If I needed any further proof Jackie was an oddball however, it came the following Saturday when we played Blackburn Rovers away, and to my surprise she asked me if she could come with me.

"Certainly not," I replied.

"Why not?"

"Because hooliganism is a man thing. Not something that should concern the ladies."

Well she looked crestfallen and I can't say I blamed her, because if somebody had told me I couldn't go somewhere I wanted to go, I too would look crestfallen. But, all the same it had surprised me she had asked to come because I had already told her about my hooligan activities and introduced her to F-Troop, so she was perfectly aware of why we were travelling to Blackburn.

She still insisted she wanted to come with us though, so I had to put my foot down and say no.

She wouldn't have it. "But why won't you take me?" she cried, grasping my hand and looking at me pleadingly. "Why?"

"Because you're a girl and you could get hurt. What's more, it's not a pretty sight seeing grown men fighting each other. You might have nightmares."

"Oh but I won't get in the way and it will be fun watching grown men fighting each other, and who knows, once you've beaten them up I can step in and dish out some punishment of my own." With that she pulled some handcuffs out of her bag and looked at me with her lips curled up in a grin.

Well I told you she was a weirdo didn't I, and the fact that the girl was into bondage, hence the handcuffs and gag, proved it.

I had still said no and the following Saturday, F-Troop and I got the coach at six sharp for the long journey up to Blackburn.

However, I was in for a surprise because as soon as we passed Birmingham a familiar face appeared from the steps that led to a small bedroom underneath the coach, which the driver used for long journeys. My eyes nearly popped out of my head when I saw who it was.

"What the fuck are you doing here?" I cried, once I had got over the shock.

"I've come to help you take care of the Blackburn firm," Jackie dangled her now infamous handcuffs in front of me with a grin.

Well the rest of the lads burst out laughing as indeed did I and in fact the whole thing was just so ridiculous, that it took us ages to regain our composure.

When we did, I looked at her with a tear in my eye and said, "How the fuck did you get on the coach anyway?"

"Oh but Walter let me on."

"Walter?" I said surprised.

"Yes the driver. He even said I could get a few hours sleep in his bed as we drove here."

"Oh aye," I said glancing over at the old git who was looking at me nervously through his windscreen mirror. "And why would he do that?"

"Well," she said, curling her lips into a grin again and dangling the handcuffs, "it's amazing what men will do when I have these on me, really amazing."

At Blackburn we did what we always do when we arrived at our destination, which was to get off at the town centre and make our way to the nearest pub. In this case it just happened to be right next to the train station, so it wasn't long before Blackburn's firm the Mill Hill Mob located us and made their presence known. I was delighted because I was looking forward to a good scrap, but just as both firms were squaring off and I was about to yell *Awooooooo*, their top boy stepped forward with a frown on his face.

"Hey up," he said, "you've got a girl in your midst."

I spun round and then shook my head in disbelief. That stupid bitch Riley was standing there glaring at us when I had told her to stay inside the pub to avoid getting hurt.

"You," I said, pointing an angry finger at her. "Get back inside that pub now, things are about to kick off."

My words did not have the desired effect. She just came running over with a smile on her face. "Oh but I want to stay Harry because as I told you before, once you've finished with the Blackburn firm I intend to deal out a bit of punishment of my own." With that she pulled a whipping stick out of her bag and I withered in embarrassment.

Blackburn's top boy gasped and Riley continued... "Yes I intend to deal out punishment of my own."

She patted the whipping stick in her hand again and both firms looked at each other and then burst out laughing and started to roll about.

I was in hysterics too as was their top boy, and once I had regained my composure again, I said to him, "I'm sorry mate, I told her she couldn't come with us, but she sneaked on the coach and we didn't know she was there until we got past Birmingham."

"No worries mate. But where did you find her. Rampton?"

"You would think so wouldn't you," I replied with a grin, "because she's certainly certifiable, but no I didn't find her at Rampton, but down at the local pub."

He laughed, and after that we piled into the pub and had a drink together – F-Troop and the Mill Hill Mob. Sounds odd I know, but what else could we do. We were too busy laughing at the day's events to do anything else.

BOLTON WANDERERS

The next week, we were playing Bolton Wanderers at home and I was really looking forward to this, because Bolton's Cuckoo Boys were said to have a decent crew who could hold their own against any firm, no matter what the odds.

However, these bozos got pissed at Piccadilly Station and ended up catching the train to Scotland instead of London and so the fight did not go ahead.

I told you hooligan firms were full of dickheads, didn't I?

PLYMOUTH ARGYLE

The following week we played Plymouth Argyle away and that turned out to be better than expected, because as soon as their firm spotted us they came storming over and laying into us with all guns blazing.

I was surprised, because Plymouth's firm, the Casual Element, were not considered a decent outfit back then, and in fact they were considered a bit of a joke in the hooligan world because of their reputation of running away rather than standing their ground when confronted by a rival firm.

Or so I was told, but it was all a load of baloney – well at least it was today – because not only were they standing their ground, but they were also pushing us back. We were in danger of getting a good hiding, but then the sound of police sirens waded through the air and I watched as they backed off before legging it down the street and eventually out of sight.

So, the Casual Element put in a good performance but don't be fooled. They weren't getting the better of us because they were harder than we were, but because they were fighting on their own turf and had superior numbers, as those fighting on their own turf often do. However, whatever the reason, we also fled the scene because those police sirens were getting louder and louder and we had no intention of being arrested by the boys in blue.

The funny thing about that day though was Jackie Rylie was with us again. As I said before, hooligans never took their girls along with them on match days and for obvious reasons, but she was different and I could not resist bringing her along just for the sheer fun of it. Indeed, she was so funny that it would have been silly not to because of the things she did and said.

I've told you before that Jackie was heavily into bondage but what I haven't told you is that she was also a goth and liked to dress all in black, wear black lipstick and cover her eyelashes in black too, making her look like death's younger sister. She also liked to don a witch's hat and broom making her look even more like something from a freak show, which was quite funny because as soon as we headed over to Plymouth's ground and entered the stadium the Plymouth fans burst out laughing.

"Feeling all right love?"

"The circus's in town is it?"

We couldn't do anything about that as there were hordes of police officers between their supporters and ours. However, all that changed when we entered the stand where the rest of the Millwall fans were.

"How you doing darling?" cried a freckle-faced man with ginger hair. "Looking to cast a spell over the opposition are you?"

"Hush Bobby," said a youth standing next to him nervously. "That's Harry the Dog she's with."

"What the guy who tore into the Bristol fans single-handedly?"

His mate nodded.

"And the one who turned up at some NF member's house with a shotgun threatening to blow their head off?"

"That's him."

"Bloody hell," he cried, "I've heard about him."

He looked at me with a look of admiration on his face and I had to smile to myself because it was just another sign my name was starting to become infamous in hooligan circles and I wasn't complaining. In fact I was loving every moment of it because when you're eighteen years old and involved in the hooligan scene and people know who you are, and look upon you with a mixture of trepidation and fear, it does wonders for your ego. It certainly did wonders for mine and as I say I was loving every moment of it.

After the game, it was my intention to challenge their top boy to a one-on-one given we could not defeat them in a gang ruck, but it was a waste of time as the police herded all of the Millwall fans together and escorted us back to the coaches.

Still it wasn't all doom and gloom, because as the coach left Plymouth and hit the motorway, Jackie, to everybody's amusement, took her clothes of and began strutting her stuff up and down the aisle. That was before she insisted on sitting on the back seat and flashing her credentials to any passing motorist.

I told you the girl was one hell of a weirdo didn't I?

LUTON TOWN

Over the next few weeks we had fights with Leyton Orient's firm the Orient Transit Firm, Charlton Athletics B-Mob, and Fulham's Thames Valley Travellers and I can't say they were anything to shout about given the police had everything under control and we were confined to yelling abuse at each other and not much else. Then we got Luton away and all that changed.

We set off about eleven in the morning, and as soon as we arrived, we made a beeline to the nearest pub to await the arrival of Luton's firm the MIGs, hoping they had scouts in the town who would soon locate our whereabouts.

We weren't disappointed. We barely had time to order our drinks before one of our spotters burst in and said there was a horde of lads running our way. We immediately dashed out to confront them, but then stopped dead in our tracks.

The lads running towards us were brown skinned and dark-haired and we all looked at each other thinking this can't be Luton's firm surely, because apart from the Chelsea Head Hunters no other hooligan firm in England had more links to the NF than they did. We were right, they weren't the MIGs. They were Asians and they were just as surprised to see us, because the minute they did, they stopped dead in their tracks and I heard one cry out in an Asian accent, "Oh bloody hell, they're in front of us too."

I was just wondering to whom they were referring, when I heard a lot of yelling and screaming behind them and hordes of white youths came flying round the corner yelling, "Pakis out" and clutching an assortment of weapons. I took one look at them and knew instantly that they were Luton's mob, not just because of the racist chants, but because many of them were wearing Luton shirts. They too stopped dead when they saw us and I heard one of them yell, "Fuck me it's F-Troop."

I laughed and wanted to lay into them there and then, but the Asian lads were in the way, so I told F-Troop to stand aside to let them pass before turning back to Luton's mob and yelling, "Awoooooooo."

The Luton mob were surprised, but not as surprised as they were when I went dashing over and jumped into the lot of them. There were yells of "Lunatic" and "Madman" but I couldn't care less about that; or the fact that F-Troop were just standing there, looking on in astonishment. All I did care about was decking as many of them as I could and so one after another they hit the deck.

Then I heard somebody cry, "Fuck me that guy must be Harry the Dog."

"Harry the Dog," yelled another, "you mean Harry the Poodle. I heard Mickey Crane knocked him out with one punch."

There was laughter all round and I spun round and saw this skinhead standing there with a grin on his face. I knew immediately he was their top boy from his demeanour, but before he could do anything I punched him so hard in the face he virtually flew through the air and crashed to the ground with blood gushing out of his nose. I wasn't finished yet. Lurching forward I lifted his head and began smacking him in the face over and over again.

"Now listen to me, you Nazi bastard," I yelled. "That fucking wimp Mickey Crane only got the better of me because he took me by surprise. He didn't have the guts to face me head on, because he knew he would wind up in intensive care just like that miserable brother of his. So you and your Nazi bozos can go back and tell him I'll be having a word in his ear when he comes out of prison."

With that I booted him hard in the head, causing more blood to gush out of his nose and then picked him up and threw him head first into the Luton mob.

"Awoooooooo," I yelled as he crashed on top of some of them. "Awoooooooo," I yelled as the rest turned on their heels and fled in terror.

DANI LIA

It's a funny thing, but now I am in my sixties, one question I always get asked by today's generation of hooligans is, "Apart from you Harry, who was the hardest hooligan in your day?" Well my answer always surprises them because they expect me to say Cass Pennant, Calton Leach, or some other pathetic wanker with a big name, so they are gobsmacked when I say, "Dani Lia!" ... even though he really was the hardest bastard at the time.

In fact Dani was so hard he could knock you out with one punch; as many a hooligan found out. He was the top boy of Wigan Athletics firm, the Wigan Goon Squad. To get that role he had brazenly walked into the pub where the Goon Squad were drinking and informed them he was taking over the leadership of the firm and anybody who had a problem with that would get the crap beaten out of them.

The events that followed saw three of the Wigan firm on the floor and out for the count, another pinned to the wall with a ninja star nailed through his hand, and Dani, well he was recognised as the new leader of the Wigan Goon Squad.

But Dani wasn't just the hardest hooligan there ever lived, he was the smartest. He had a genius level intellect and would come up with all sorts of ingenious ways to stop a rival firm entering his territory and taking liberties as I myself found out.

We were playing Hull away and to get there by train meant changing at Crew, and as soon as the train stopped, I jumped out and stormed down the platform with the rest of F-Troop behind me.

My plan was to get a kebab or something else to eat because our connecting train wasn't due in for another half an hour, but that changed after an old man came rushing up to me waving his walking stick in the air as he did.

"I say," he cried, "are you Harry the Dog?"

"Yeah," I growled. "Why?"

"I have a message from the Vale Lunatic Fringe."

"What fucking message?"

"They said to tell you they are in the pub across the road and if you dare show your face they will cut your tongue out of your head and see to it that you howl no more."

"What?"

I should have chinned him there and then but given his age I thought better of it and went over and stormed into the pub.

"Awoooooooo," I cried as I went steaming into the Vale Lunatic Fringe. "Awoooooooo," I cried after I had knocked many of them out and the rest had turned and fled for their lives.

It was fantastic stuff but I would not have been in such a jubilant mood had I realised that the whole thing was a set up and the old man was none other than Dani Lia in disguise. He wanted the Vale Lunatic Fringe out of action because Port Vale were playing Wigan away that day, and he didn't want them entering his turf and causing mischief so he used me to do it.

How exactly he did this and how he knew I would be at Crew on that day is something you can read all about in his excellent biography, *Dani Lia, Diary of a Football Hooligan and The Wigan Goon Squad's Top Boy*. But he certainly tricked me and it was only many years later that I realised it.

I told you he was the smartest hooligan that I had ever met didn't I?

HATCHET HARRY

The only other football hooligan I ever rated was Hatchet Harry of the Derby Lunatic Fringe (DLF) fame, who like Dani Lia was active at the same time I was. Unlike Dani our paths never crossed, which is just as well because Harry was a psychopath in every sense of the word, and God knows what would have happened if we had met.

I'm not going to say too much about Harry because his book *Hatchett Harry, Football Hooligan and Derby Lunatic Fringe (DLF) thug* is out on Amazon and you can read about it there. All I will say is that the book has poor reviews, because those who have read it say the book is too far-fetched and the things he writes about could not possibly have happened – yet they did.

He really did attack his opponents with hatchets and he really did behead two in the process.

HEREFORD UNITED

The following week we played Carlisle United at home and Jackie Rylie was with us again. However, it turned out to be a disappointing day because Carlisle's mob, the Border City Firm never bothered to show up, and I discovered later that it was because most of them had been to a twenty-first birthday bash the night before and were too pissed to make the journey to the Den. That was a pity because I had been looking forward to kicking the hell out of them.

The week after that we were playing Hereford United away, which meant another long journey up north and Jackie was one of the first to board the coach. She wasn't an early bird so to speak, and neither was I, so it wasn't long before we were asleep in the small bedroom underneath the coach and it was a good thing too, because today would turn out to be one like no other.

It began when the coach started to experience engine problems just outside Tewkesbury and the driver had to pull into a service station before it broke down altogether. I was fuming, particularly when the driver said there was no way that the coach could go anywhere until a mechanic could come up from London to fix it and that would take hours.

"What the fuck are we supposed to do until then, sleep?"

"If you want to you can, although if you're hungry, why don't you go into the motorway café over there and get something to eat, or get a newspaper to read while you wait."

I give him a look. "And what about the game. We're going to miss it aren't we?"

He nodded.

That was frustrating, but there was nothing I could do about it so some of us trailed over to the café to get a bite to eat and to while away the time as we did.

I say some of us, because as always on these occasions booze was plentiful and by now many of the lads were so pissed they were out for the count and just sat there with stupid expressions on their faces. So, all in all there were eight of us who headed off to the café, me, Jackie, Robo, Simsey, Winto, Ginger Tom, and the Kitson twins who were new to the firm with this being only their second outing.

I have to admit visiting the café was a good thing, because I was absolutely famished and it wasn't long before I was doing justice to some excellent bacon and eggs washed down by excellent coffee. In fact I enjoyed it so much I even had a second helping and was looking forward to sleeping it off, when I heard the sound of sirens wailing through the air and before I knew it police vans were pulling up everywhere and police officers were jumping out.

"What the fuck." I rushed outside and my eyes nearly popped out of my head. There were numerous bodies lying on the ground and I could tell without asking that those who had remained on our coach had been involved in a skirmish of some sort. Not only were they blooded and bruised, some were lying motionless and were clearly unconscious.

I yelled to Bomber, "What the fuck happened here?"

"We got jumped by Aldershot Town's A Company," he replied. "They pulled up and the minute they spotted us they attacked without warning. Most of us were too pissed to put up much resistance."

I shook my head and made my way back into the café. Why oh why these bozos insisted on getting drunk when they knew full well they were only making the journey to take part in a ruck against a rival firm, is anybody's guess, but they had and I didn't have the slightest bit of sympathy for them. So instead, I rang up for a taxi to take the eight of us to the nearest train station, which as it happened turned out to be Tewkesbury Central.

At Tewkesbury we were in luck. The train to London was in and it wasn't long before we were hurtling through the Gloucestershire countryside on the way back to the city we had left a few hours earlier. I was still fuming about the day's events and said as much.

Then one of the Kitson twins said to me, "How did that happen Harry? How did Aldershot's firm just come across us like that?"

"Purely by luck mate," I replied bitterly. "They must have been on their way to a game and pulled into the motorway service station to get some grub and spotted us purely by chance. So they attacked our coach and you can't really blame them. I would have done the same myself." I would have done too if I'd had the chance.

Then, this pompous buffoon in a pinstriped suit reading the Daily Mail leaned over and said, "Do you mind shutting it son I am trying to read my paper."

"You fucking what?"

"I said do you mind shutting it son, as I'm trying to read my paper."

I got up and punched him so hard he fell back and was completely out, but I wasn't finished yet. This guy had pissed me off and I wanted to hurt him so much that I went to strike him again, even though he was already away with the fairies.   However, Jackie stepped in, and said, "Don't Harry let me deal with him."

I sat back in my seat as Jackie took charge of the situation and I have to admit I am glad that she did, because what she did was quite funny.

First she delved into his pockets and pulled out his wallet, which was bulging with bank notes of various denominations. "Thank you kind sir," she said kissing the unconscious man on the lips and putting his wallet in her jacket, "that will pay for a nice meal and lots of other extras later."

Then she took the gold watch off his wrist, followed by an expensive ring, and again kissed him on his lips before putting the items in her pocket and thanking him for his kind generosity again.

You may wonder what the other passengers thought of all this, but the truth was there weren't many in the carriage and those who were, just happened to be elderly and were sitting further up the train oblivious to the whole thing.

It was just as well, because Riley then kissed the unconscious man again, only this time long and lingeringly, before loosening his tie. For a moment I thought she was going to undress him and rape him. I certainly wouldn't have put it past her. But as it happens, she didn't. She just loosened his tie before taking her black lipstick out of her bag and applying it to his lips and eyelashes. When she had finished he looked more of a freak than she did. It was so funny I could not stop laughing.

Half an hour later, the train pulled into London Euston and we all got off, all that is except the man in the pinstriped suit. He was still away with the fairies, but Jackie had arranged it to make it look as though he was asleep and so nobody bothered him as they got off the train. They might however, have wondered why a well-dressed man in his fifties was wearing black lipstick and painted eyelashes.

It was the same with the passengers who got on the train and a few minutes later we watched as the doors shut and the train continued on towards Plymouth, its final destination.

Jackie waved the train away and then turned to me with a smile. "Well that was fun," she said taking the cash out of his wallet and transferring it to her purse. "Now let's go and enjoy a first-class meal courtesy of that kind sir back there."

With that she walked over to the taxi rank after discarding the empty wallet in the trash as she did.

PANORAMA

A few days later, I was fast asleep in bed when my mum knocked on the door and said I was wanted on the phone.

As soon as I picked it up a well-bred voice said, "Harry the Dog?"

"Yeah," I growled.

"I'm Patrick Dewry from the BBC's current affairs programme Panorama. Would it be possible if you could come to the studios so we can have a word with you? We're doing an exposé on football hooliganism and would like to interview you in relation to the issue."

Well I thought it was a bloody joke and said so, but it turned out that it wasn't and before I knew it journalists from Panorama were following the rest of F-Troop and me around the country as we took on firm after firm.

To be honest it was exciting, but not as exciting as when the documentary was broadcast to the nation in August 1977 and everybody saw my handsome mug on their television screens telling people what it was like being a football hooligan.

"All we go for is a good game of football, a good punch up, and a good piss up," I told the reporters as our coach hurtled up the M1 on our way to deal with Nottingham Forrest firm the Forrest Executive Crew.

"The whole purpose of being a football hooligan," I told the same journalist a week later, "is to engage in fists fights with like-minded firms and show we are the hardest mob around, which we are, as the Burnley Suicide Squad are about to find out today."

As I said, it was exciting stuff and for days afterwards people kept stopping me in the street and telling me how much they enjoyed the programme and what a star they thought I was. Some of them even wanted their picture taken with me just to show they had met me, so in a funny way I became a bigger celebrity amongst hooligans and ordinary Millwall fans than I was before.

When the football season was over, I took myself off to Tenerife with the rest of the lads to relax and chill out, because back in the seventies that was the place to go when you wanted to have fun even though Jackie Rylie insisted on coming with us.

I said to her, "Look babe, I can understand why you want to come with us because you're worried aren't you? You're worried that all the girls will be after my body, given I'm such a handsome hunk and one hell of a catch?"

But she just burst out laughing and said, "Don't flatter yourself Harry; I'm coming because I want a holiday myself and don't worry about the girls. You can have as many as you like. In fact I will be having a few myself. I like girls too you know."

Well I nearly choked on my drink when she said that, because I had never considered she might be bisexual up until then, but then she did have a very healthy sexual appetite so it shouldn't have come as much as a surprise as it did.

So there I was, night after night, shagging girl after girl and she didn't even bat an eyelid. Mind you I can't say I blame her because she wasn't in a position to say anything herself was she, what with her shagging every male or female she took a fancy to.

That said she was determined to get her fun in other ways and when the mood was upon her, she would glare at some lad and give him the big come on and then when he came up to her she would slap him across the face and say, "How dare you. I'm with my boyfriend. What kind of girl do you think I am?"

Well the consequences of that were inevitable. He would turn to me, I would turn to him, and fists would fly. I say fists would fly, but not for long because most of the people I fought couldn't punch a hole in a paper bag and one after one they hit the floor with blood gushing out of their noses. In fact I decked so many people that the locals named me the *Toro Furioso*, the Raging Bull which made me laugh to say the least, but brought with it whole loads of trouble in the process.

We were in the bar one night, when this prat walked in and stormed over to me. He was wearing a large white vest with black tracksuit bottoms and trainers and judging by his stocky physique and bulging muscles I guessed he was a bodybuilder of some sort.

"You the Englishman they call the Toro Furioso?"

"Yeah," I cried, glancing briefly at the three guys and pretty blond he was with, before turning back to him with a growl on his face. "What of it?"

He poked me in the chest, "Well you're not a Toro Furioso ... you're a big pussy cat. At least that is, compared to me."

He raised his arms to show off his muscles and I stepped forward to chin him but Jackie's voice cut through the air.

"No Harry wait. I want to feel his muscles."

She stepped forward and gently began feeling them as we all glared at her in disbelief. For a few seconds she continued to feel them before turning away and saying to me with a grin.

"Well he's certainly a big boy Harry. Now beat him up and I will take it from there."

With that the man gasped, his girlfriend went red and I punched him full on in the face sending him backwards and over a table. His buddies looked shocked, but with Robo and the lads looking on could do nothing but watch helplessly as the goon picked himself up and came at me with all guns blazing, before ramming his head into my chest and sending me wheeling backwards into a wall.

Within seconds, he had thrown his huge arms around me and lifted me off my feet, and I tried to punch him but he had my arms trapped. So, I headbutted him instead and when he dropped me, I headbutted him again and again and again. But still the bastard would not go down.

Not only that, but somehow he landed a right hook on my cheek which sent me backwards and I recoiled in disbelief before surging forward and punching him in the gob. He was battered and bruised but he was still not down, so I followed through with a left hook to his jaw, before hitting him with a series of punches to his ribs. This brought him to his knees, and I then followed through with a kick to the head and that was it he was out for the count.

I thought some of the locals might kick off and turn on me but they didn't. Instead they clapped wildly, and so I stood with my arms in the air before throwing my head back and yelling, "Awoooooooo," with delight.

Jackie too was delighted and to my surprise went up to the man's girlfriend, who was looking at me admiringly even though I had just beaten up her boyfriend, and started chatting to her saying she hoped there were no hard feelings.

There obviously weren't because somehow she managed to persuade the girl to come back to the hotel where all of us engaged in a threesome. I told you Tenerife was the place to have fun didn't I?

LEWISHAM

A few days after we got back, Robo came to see me and said, "Harry, how would you like to be involved in another ruck?"

"Would love it," I replied, "but the football season doesn't start until next month so how can we?"

"Because the NF are holding a march in Lewisham next week and I thought you would like to come. All the NF top boys will be there and anti-fascists will be there to greet them."

"Can't wait."

On the day of the march we made our way to Lewisham by coach, which didn't take us long as it was only two miles away and in no time at all the coach was pulling into a large car park along with hundreds of other coaches alongside us.

I turned to Robo, "I know you said there would be lots of people here but I wasn't expecting this many. There must be hundreds of people, if not thousands. Where the hell have they all come from?"

"From all over the country," he said with a grin. "The NF are bussing in people from all over and so are the anti-fascists."

He wasn't kidding, because as I glanced around I could see there were people of all ages, creeds, and colours here and many of them were carrying placards which read: *Scousers Against Racism*, or *Brummies Against Racism*, or *Geordies Against Racism*.

It was fantastic stuff, particularly when I saw the hordes of ANL protestors waving their yellow and black placards, but I was slightly apprehensive. I thought to myself if the NF do kick off and storm into this lot then I doubt they would put up much resistance because many of them were spotty face students or middle-class lefties who looked like they would blow over in the wind. Still with me here, along with the rest of F-Troop, the NF would be very foolish to start anything, because if they did we would finish it and in a way they would definitely understand.

Like Bermondsey, Lewisham was another of those places I had never been to before despite its close proximity to Millwall, and, like Milllwall, it had its fair share of immigrants from Africa, Asia, and the Caribbean. In fact as we continued down the street you would have thought we were in the Caribbean with the number of West Indians I saw standing on the pavement smoking weed and dancing away to music provided by a group of colourful Rastafarians.

I said to Robo, "Bloody hell that's a good tune... they should be on Top of the Pops."

He laughed. "You're right Harry they should."

Then we stopped dead in our tracks. A group of lads were walking our way, all white and mostly skinheads, and I thought fuck me the NF are here. This took some brass because there were only around thirty of them, and forty of us with hordes of blacks and anti-fascists either side of them. In fact, one or two of the blacks were already giving them strange looks.

"Do they have a suicide wish or what?"

"Possibly Harry," he replied, "but I think this lot is the NF Leader Guard. The hardest and best street fighters on the far right."

"Ah yes," I said smashing my fist in my hand. Mickey Crane leads them doesn't he? Well it's a pity the little faggot is still banged up in his prison cell, because if he was here I would put him in intensive care like his wimp of a brother."

He laughed and I stepped forward to confront the skinheads.

"You lot," I cried taking them by surprise. "If you racist bastards thought you could just come here and take liberties, you're seriously deluded."

With that I threw my head back and yelled, "Awoooooooo," before running over to confront them.

I was in for a surprise though, because instead of putting their fists up and getting ready to defend themselves as you might expect them to do, their leader put his hand up.

"Whoa! We're not racists mate, we're Red Action. We hate the fascists as much as you do. Don't we Winston?" He glanced over at one of the Rastafarians and the latter came swaggering over with a trumpet in his hands.

"Ya man," he replied. "These guys fight fascists all over the place. Top guys they are."

He wasn't kidding, because although I had never met anybody from Red Action I had heard of them and knew that they were one of the most violent anti-racist groups in the country and one of the most feared.

They were formed in 1974, despite *Wikipedia* claiming it was 1981, and unlike the ANL believed that the best way to fight the *fash* as they called the fascists was to do so in a way they understood, by breaking up their meetings, attacking them in their homes, and smashing baseball bats over their heads. I could well understand that, because if I was fighting fascists every week, I would have done the same. So, they had my full respect.

But, I am not going to say too much about them here because Dave Hann and Steve Tizley have written an excellent book on Red Action's activities called, *No Retreat, The Secret War Between Britain's Anti-Facists and the Far Right* and you can read all about it there.

However, I will say this, if I had been anything other than a football hooligan and leading F-Troop at the time, I may well have joined Red Action. I liked their politics, methods, and the violence they meted out on the NF and other like-minded Nazi scumbags.

Back to the march ... once we had established that we were all on the same side, barriers came tumbling down, and one of their number came over and said, "Aren't you Harry the Dog?"

"Yeah," I cried puzzled. "How do you know?"

"That whooooo you gave before, mate," he replied grinning. "I recognised it. You're the guy who put Mickey Crane's brother in hospital aren't you, after turning up at his house with a shotgun looking for Crane himself?"

I smiled and was just about to reply when I heard somebody yell, "The fash are coming ... the fash are coming."

They didn't need to say it, because just then hordes of police officers appeared out of nowhere and the carnival-like atmosphere ceased and everybody stood on the pavement looking down the street waiting for the NF to appear.

We didn't have long to wait, because very soon a figure appeared down the road holding a Union Jack and I said to Robo, "Who the fuck is that, Colonel Blimp?" With his tall majestic figure and smart appearance he was the spitting image of him.

Robo just laughed and said, "No mate that's John Tyndall the Chairman of the NF."

"What that wanker?" I yelled, and with such venom that the man turned to me and muttered something under his breath. Then I caught sight of the hordes of tough-looking skinheads wearing their white shirts, jeans, and Dr Marten boots walking behind him, and I said to Robo, "Is that them? Is that the infamous Leader Guard?"

He nodded and I was just about to yell wankers, when the crowd began yelling, "Nazi scum of our street ... Nazi scum of our street."

I watched as some neo-Nazi buffoon who had been leading the scumbags turned to the crowd and yelled, "Oh aye, want to take me on do you, then come on then. I'm Mickey Crane I'm the best street fighter on the far right. I'll take you on."

I stared at him in disbelief, for up until then I hadn't recognised him. I had thought the bastard was in prison, but he wasn't, he was here and I wasn't going to miss the opportunity of putting him in intensive care.

I threw my head back and yelled, "Awoooooooo," but before I could rush over and lay into him, events overtook me as mass brawls began breaking out up and down the NF lines as anti-fascists began tearing into them.

In fact it was pandemonium, particularly as the NF lines stretched back as far as the eye could see. Before I knew it I was laying out one NF member after another and not just members of the Leader Guard, but other NF bozos who got in my way including one overweight buffoon with a tattoo on his face, who I punched in the face, kicked in the balls, and then stamped on the head, leaving him flat out on the ground.

But my main concern was finding Mickey Crane, even though I had lost sight of the bastard and the police were running around like headless chickens trying to restore order. I continued to punch, kick, headbutt, and if necessary jump on the head of any NF who got in my way and I was actually enjoying myself and hoping the day would never end.

Then I spotted Crane. He was laying into a group of blacks and looked as though he was enjoying himself too, what with the way he was headbutting, kicking, and knocking out anyone who got in his way. Clearly the man could fight and a lot of the anti-fascists were backing away from him warily.

But it didn't impress me and I pushed my way over to him before yelling, "Awooooooo," again and again. As Crane spun round in astonishment, I punched him so hard he flew through the air before smashing into a lamppost and sliding down and out for the count.

"Awooooooo," I cried as the NF looked at me in surprise.

"Awooooooo," I cried as a BBC camera crew, which had appeared out of nowhere, filmed me, and then Crane as he lay there senseless.

"Awooooooo," I cried as the NF began backing away from me hastily.

"Awooooooo," I cried as lots of girls came over and began kissing me on the cheek.

BERNIE O'CONNER

The next day, the newspapers were full of the story with many calling it *the Battle of Lewisham* and boasting how the NF had come to Lewisham to spread their message of hate and been given a good hiding in the process.

I say many, but it was not a view shared by some of the more right-wing papers. Many of them claimed that the NF had been exercising their democratic right to protest and been met by hordes of left-wing thugs with fists, boots, and bottles in the process. *"Clearly, many of these so call anti-fascists were nothing more than a bunch of left-wing boot boys bordering the lunatic fringe,"* wrote one.

I was amused by that, but nowhere near as amused as when I saw the news that night and there I was on everybody's television screen punching Crane to kingdom come and then yelling, "Awoooooooo," as he lay motionless alongside the lamppost. In fact I was delighted, because I knew that anyone watching it would now know I had beaten the NF's top boy and put him in his place and he had been very foolish to take on Harry the Dog, very foolish indeed.

I could not afford to be complacent; however, because I knew Crane would want his revenge and it was only a matter of time before he came looking for it. I thought fuck it, I'll find out where the little runt is and go round and blow his fucking head off.

Before I could do anything though, the phone rang and when I picked it up a well-bred voice said, "Harry the Dog?"

"Yeah," I replied, gripping the phone tighter, thinking it was some Nazi scumbag about to give me a tirade of abuse. "Who the fuck is this?"

"My name is Joey Porter and I'm a businessman here in London. Perhaps you've heard of me?"

Heard of him... who the fuck had not? The man was a legend in underworld circles and with good reason. He had been the best man at Ronnie Kray's wedding and was thought by the police to have been behind several murders, although he had never been convicted of any. Indeed, the police not only believed he was guilty of murder, but of extortion, prostitution, and illegal gambling, even though the man had never so much as received a parking ticket.

I had once heard it said he was the modern day Professor Moriarty of crime in so much as nothing went on in London without him knowing about it, and without his say so, and while that maybe a slight exaggeration, it certainly shows the esteem to which this man was held in criminal circles.

That said, I still wanted to know why he was ringing me and he went on to explain that amongst his many business interests was boxing and unlicensed fights, which sounded fascinating particularly when he said he wanted to arrange an unlicensed fight between me and Mickey Crane.

He said he had seen the TV footage of me knocking Crane out and heard that the man had knocked me out during a previous encounter and he thought it would be a good money-spinner to arrange another fight. When I asked him what he meant by money-spinner his answer virtually blew me away.

"£10,000 to you and your opponent" he replied, "with the winner getting another £10,000."

"£10,000?" I gasped.

"Yes, £10,000."

"With the winner getting another £10,000 you say?"

"Yep."

Bloody hell, that was real money back then – £20,000 was enough money to buy a house and still have cash in your pocket, so I said yes and he said he would arrange it and get back to me in due course.

So off to work I went with a spring in my step dying to tell the O'Conner brothers all about it. To my surprise they already knew, because it turned out that Joey Porter was so confident that both Crane and me would agree to the fight, he had already set things in motion and contacted Bernie O'Conner to host it and Bernie was not only their great-uncle but a living legend.

In fact he had been a bare-knuckle champion in his youth and had once held the title of King of the Gypsies, after beating the best the gypsy community could offer.

What the man did not know about fighting was not worth knowing as I soon discovered when the O'Conner brothers drove me over to North London to meet him two days later.

He was a giant of a man, six foot five and as strong as an ox despite being in his fifties, and the minute I saw him I knew we would get on and not just because of his hearty manner and sense of humour, but also his plain speaking.

"Listen Harry," he said once the introductions were over, "I'll put it to you plainly. Joey Porter has asked me to stage the fight here and I'm willing to do that, but I am going to take you under my wing and teach you everything I know about fighting, because I hate Nazis and I don't want that Nazi bastard to win."

When he said he hated Nazis he wasn't kidding as I soon found out when he took me into his caravan and showed me his photo album. It contained pictures of his dead grandparents and other family members who had suffered at the hands of the Nazis.

When people think of the Nazi death camps they think of Jews and the terrible crimes committed in them in places like Treblinka Sobibor and Auschwitz. I'm not saying they shouldn't, but what many people don't realise is that others perished in the camps too, including gays, Communists and other political undesirables such as gypsies, who were sent to the gas chambers in their thousands and gassed like the rest of them.

Bernie had told me he was going to take me under his wing and teach me all about fighting and he wasn't kidding. Even though I was a hard bastard, I wasn't in Bernie's league and over the next few weeks he taught me everything he knew about fighting, including how to get out of a headlock, defend yourself if you're in a headlock, and how to defend yourself when you're on the ground. It was fun, but that wasn't the end of the excitement.

Bernie may have been the wrong side of 50, but he was still able to pull the girls and by God he did. He lived on a massive gypsy camp on the outskirts of Barnet and it seemed that half the women who lived there were his for the taking, because in the evenings he would be in his caravan shagging one of them one night, and two of them the next.

Even Jackie Rylie got in on the act. She came with me on my many trips to the camp and it wasn't long before she was bedding Bernie and adding the former King of the Gypsies to her list of conquests. I wasn't complaining though, because while he was making hay with my girlfriend, I was bedding his wife and loving every moment of it. I told you it was fun being around Bernie didn't I?

FIGHT

On the day of the fight, I was picked up by the O'Conner brothers and driven to Bernie's camp where I was introduced to Joey Porter. He shook my hand warmly and told me how much he was looking forward to the fight.

"Not as much as I am," I grinned.

He smiled and went on to tell me that over half a million pounds had been placed on the fight with Crane the favourite to win."

"Crane is?" I said surprised.

He nodded.

"And half a million you say?"

He nodded again.

I pulled myself up straight. "Well those who have betted on Crane are going to lose their money," I said with a burgeoning smile, "because I'm going to knock him out again."

He smiled and ten minutes later I made my way to the ring where the fight was to take place. The so-called ring was nothing more than a large square in a field, with chairs placed around it and dodgy looking characters sitting in them, smoking cigars, and talking.

I say dodgy looking characters, but in reality they were nothing more than a who's who of London's villains, with a variety of con men, drug dealers, and other lowlifes behind them and more behind them still.

Jackie Rylie was there too, and the minute she saw me she began jumping up and down and yelling my name, as did the whole of F-Troop who had turned up to support me.

Mickey Crane was also there and the minute he clapped eyes on me; his face hardened, and he narrowed his eyes. He was a vicious-looking character and with his familiar denim jeans, Doc Martens, white top and braces, he looked every bit the Nazi thug I knew he was.

With me now in the ring, the atmosphere changed and you could not have heard a pin drop.

Crane came storming over with his fists raised and I threw my head back in the air before yelling "Awoooooooo," and then storming into him.

With my first punch I sent the bastard backwards and tumbling on to the grass, but he was soon back on his feet and hitting me with a volley of punches to my head, body, and face.

"Bloody hell," I thought. "This guy's fast" and I threw a right hook, but he ducked under it and again hit me with a volley of punches and this time causing my nose to bleed.

With the blood gushing and the crowd looking on, Crane thought he was winning, but it's one thing drawing blood but another putting your opponent out of action, and for the next ten minutes we went at it hammer and tongs as the punches continued to fly thick and fast through the air.

Indeed by now, the fists were flying so fast that the scene around me was beginning to resemble one from Gladiators, with people jumping up and down and urging us both to go in for the kill.

"Knock him out Harry," yelled one.

"Deck him now Mickey," cried another.

F-Troop and the hordes of NF skinheads were also yelling encouragement to their respective top boy, and casting angry glances at the others in the process, but it was the girls who were doing the loudest yelling.

On my side, Jackie was jumping up and down and calling on me to, "Beat this 'orrible man up so I can step in and mete out punishment of my own."

On Crane's side was his cousin Michaela Crane, who I had never seen or heard of before. She later became known as the governess, because she fought and beat every female bare-knuckle fighter in the country who dared to challenge her.

Neither of them could be sure which way the fight would go, however, because Crane was still ducking and diving and hitting me with punch after punch, and I was still landing a few good punches of my own, resulting in his nose spouting blood and evening up the score.

In fact, both of us were getting in some good kicks and headbutts, and the crowd got wilder and the blood gushed faster, but I don't care who you are, nobody can keep fighting forever … no matter how fit you are.

In fact most people tire after a few minutes and the fittest of us not long after that, which is why in boxing matches fighters are given a minute's rest in between bouts to recover their strength and prevent them dropping down with exhaustion. However, this wasn't a boxing match but an unlicensed bout where rules go out the window and the fight continues until one or both of you drop.

So it wasn't a surprise that both of us were beginning to tire and the fists weren't flying as quickly as they were before. But they were still flying and I hit Crane with such a volley of punches to his body and head that I thought I had him. But, then he landed a right hook on my chin causing me to wobble, and buckle on my legs.

At that, he thought he had me and so did the crowd, but then he made the mistake of putting me in a headlock before trying to punch me in the head, and I did precisely what Bernie O'Conner had trained me to do in this situation. I brought my arm up to his face and used my fingers to push down hard on his eyes, causing him to squeal in agony and release his grip.

When he did, I stamped my foot on his knee knowing he would crash down to the floor where I could then follow through with a kick to the head… or at least that was the plan but then something unexpected happened.

When I stamped on his knee, I heard a large crack and Crane hit the floor writhing in agony. I realised I had broken the bastard's leg and I thought that would be it but it wasn't.

Somehow, the man lunged at me sending me crashing to the ground before proceeding to try to bite my ears off. I writhed in agony before thrusting my fingers into his eyes and then biting a large chuck of his ear after he released his grip.

The crowd was certainly getting their money's worth as they watched me and Crane rolling about on the ground biting, punching, and head butting each other.

I have to say I had full respect for him, then, because I had never fought anybody like him, both before or since, who had taken a beating like him but was still trading blow for blow even though he had a broken leg and could not stand on it.

But it couldn't go on. We were both exhausted, battered, and bruised, so I pushed the bastard off me, jumped to my feet, and stepped back a few paces to wipe the blood from my face and finish him once and for all.

To give him his due, the man somehow managed to get to his feet and wobbled on one foot, but the pain from his leg was now killing him and he collapsed to the ground. As he did, I rushed forward and kicked him in the head with such force that he positively flew through the air and crashed to the ground, and that was it, Crane was out and lying motionless in a pool of blood.

"Awoooooooo," I cried as the crowd began applauding wildly.

"Awoooooooo," I cried as the applause got louder and louder.

"Awoooooooo," I cried as Jackie rushed over and kissed me on my lips.

"Awoooooooo," I cried as I turned and raised my hands in a victory sign to F-Troop.

AFTERMATH

After the fight, I had enough money to go where I wanted to go and when I wanted to go there, so me and Jackie took ourselves off on a round-the-world trip to visit the Great Wall of China, the Pyramids of Egypt, the nightclubs of Paris, and the plains of Arizona, to name but a few of the places we visited.

It was fantastic and I didn't want to come back, but Jackie had only been given six months off work from the council and had to get back to England to keep her job, so back to England we came.

I returned home but not for long. Word had reached me that somebody had blasted Mickey Crane with a shotgun and the word on the street was that I had done it. There was a contract out on my life, even though I had had nothing to do with it, as Crane himself made clear when he came out of his coma a few months later. By that time, however, I was lying low in Australia and enjoying it so much I ended up staying there for forty years.

I didn't return to the country until 2017.

Robo, Simsey, and Winto were still around as indeed was Jackie Rylie and we enjoyed many a sex romp, despite the fact she was now a mistress to an MP, a member of the House of Lords, and God knows who else.

Many of the old boys in F-Troop were still around and I heard that Bomber and some of the other lads were thinking of writing a book on their hooligan days and reliving the good old times.

Mickey Crane too was thinking of writing a book as I discovered when I bumped into him by chance the other day.

He told me he was fuming because, "Some Paki called Andi Ali has written a book called *Dead Paki Walking, A Study of the British National Party (BNP)*." In the book, Ali had referred to him as a "wimp" after the two had clashed at an anti BNP protest in Millwall in June, 2003.

He was also fuming that a lot of football hooligans such as Jason Mariner, Andy Porter, and Gilly Shaw had played down their links to the far right in order to make them more likeable to their readers.

That said; I enjoy reading books by former hooligans even though some of them are full of bullshit or the author has simply got their facts wrong.

Hatchet Harry for example, recounts an incident in his book where he was told by one member of the DLF how the DLF had got the better of me in a fight in October 1970... But how could that be? I had only been 11 at the time and still in junior school. Likewise, other hooligans refer to me as Harry the Poodle but would never say so to my face.

In fact, a lot of former hooligans have written things about me they would never say to my face, but that's because I was harder than they were and they don't like to admit it. One thing was clear, however, when they write about me, they don't say I am best remembered for being a hooligan or whipping Mickey Crane, important as they are, but for my "Awoooooooo," ... just my "Awoooooooo," and nothing but my "Awoooooooo."

Printed in Great Britain
by Amazon